THE SHUFFLE

Book Two of the Jordan Saga

A Selection of Recent Titles by Terence Kelly

THE CARIB SANDS

THE GENKI BOYS

LONG LIVE THE SPY

PROPERJOHN

REVOLUTION ON ST. BARBARA

VOYAGE BEYOND BELIEF

The Jordan Saga:

THE CUT

THE SHUFFLE

THE SHUFFLE

Terence Kelly

This first world edition published in Great Britain 2000 by
SEVERN HOUSE PUBLISHERS LTD of
9–15 High Street, Sutton, Surrey SM1 1DF.
This first world edition published in the USA 2000 by
SEVERN HOUSE PUBLISHERS INC of
595 Madison Avenue, New York, N.Y. 10022.

British Library Cataloguing in Publication Data

Kelly, Terence, 1920-
The shuffle. - (The Jordan Saga ; bk. 2)
I. Title
823.9'14 [F]

ISBN 0-7278-5545-X

Typeset by Palimpsest Book Production Ltd.,
Polmont, Stirlingshire, Scotland.
Printed and bound in Great Britain by
MPG Books Ltd, Bodmin, Cornwall.

One
1927

1

"I'm coming with you, Micky."

Alice Jordan, standing in the hallway of Cranmore Hotel, in Highbury, North London, telephone receiver to her ear, fished around with her foot trying to locate and recover the shoe she'd fidgeted off because it was too tight and uncomfortable.

"Just a moment, Tom," she said. "I've kicked off my shoe and lost it."

She let the receiver dangle on its cord and bent to recover the shoe just as Colonel Wharton came down the staircase.

"Morning, Mrs Jordan! Lost something?" He had a parade-ground voice a Sergeant Major would not have been averse to possessing. He was a tall, good-looking, very well preserved man of sixty who had made something of a local name for himself by doing his bit driving a bus and helping to break last year's General Strike. He did not suffer fools gladly and was inclined to be impatient with women, especially his rather browbeaten wife – but he made an exception for Mrs Jordan and could be quoted as describing her as: 'a very pretty and sensible young woman – a damn shame there aren't a few more of them about!'

"Only my shoe, Colonel." His Christian name was Henry but he had made it clear he preferred the title.

"There's not enough damn light down here. If Bennion is too damn mean to put in a box where guests can have a conversation in privacy, then the least he can do is let them see what they're up to! I'll have a word with him."

"That would be very kind of you." She had found her shoe but delayed putting it on.

"My wife tells me you've got your boys arriving today."

"That's right, Colonel. I'll be going off to meet them at Euston shortly."

"How old are they?" He appeared quite indifferent to the fact he was interrupting a telephone conversation.

"Nine and seven."

"Never have believed it!"

He said this because he couldn't think of anything appropriate to say. It was damned difficult knowing exactly what you should say to a pretty young woman who was going through the throes of a divorce. All the more difficult when rumour had it that the husband she was divorcing was by all accounts a reasonable chap and the reason she was divorcing him was to marry this Fenwick fellow who kept turning up at Cranmore. Rum business altogether.

"They go swimming?"

Alice was momentarily baffled. "Swimming? Oh! Yes. Well, on holiday, I mean."

"Quite prepared to take 'em with me."

It was known that, winter and summer, Colonel Wharton swam every morning in the open-air swimming-pool in Highbury Fields, then ran all the way back and arrived for breakfast purple faced.

"I'll bear it in mind, Colonel," Alice said with a winning smile. "It's very good of you."

"Not at all. Any time. Be on me way."

He gave her a small salute and marched into the sitting room.

Alice put the receiver back to her ear. "Sorry about that, Tom."

She heard his chuckle. "The galloping Colonel putting everything to rights again."

"He's not a bad sort. He's just offered to take Dessy and Thady swimming."

"Yes, I heard him. No need for him to bother though. If they want to go, I'll take them."

She picked up the touch of hostility in his tone. It was absurd him being so defensive – there was no one in the world he had need to be jealous of. On the other hand it was good that he should have Dessy and Thady's interests so much at heart. He was going to be so right for them.

"Do you really want to come with me to meet them, Tom? I mean . . . do you think it's a good idea? Or wouldn't it be better for me to break it to them . . . well, gently?"

"Micky, there isn't a way of breaking it to them gently. There never was. And it's going to be very hard for you. I have to be there, beside you, helping you when you have to do it. I want them to realise that that's how it's going to be from now on. That through all the problems which life is going to have in store for us – and I mean all of us – I'm going to be there, backing *you* up and helping to sort out *their* problems. That I'm not going to be just a husband to you but a father to them. It's going to be a traumatic day for you but it isn't one we can run away from, Micky. Nor something we should put off until tomorrow. There are times in life when one has to face reality head on and this is one of them."

Yes, well, that was undeniable. With Dessy and Thady two hundred miles away in Liverpool, living happily with their grandparents, going to the same council school which she and her brothers and sisters had been to, and with Ma and Pa sworn to secrecy, she'd managed to keep what was happening from them through all these months – but now that Gibson and Weldon had confirmed that the decree nisi ought to be coming through before too long, and Tom was getting fidgety to name their wedding day, it couldn't be put off any longer. They'd expect their father to be at the station meeting them and he wouldn't be there. You could argue that she'd been wrong in keeping it from them that she was divorcing Sam and in trumping up excuses to keep them up there all this time but on balance it had seemed the better thing to do. It called for far fewer lies than would have been needed if they'd been down here living in Highbury and avoided the risk, of all things, of them bumping into their father while the proceedings were in hand. And after all, both Sam and Tom had agreed that taking it all in all it was probably better to present them with a *fait accompli* than have the fact they were going to lose their father hanging over their heads for months and months and months! Anyway rightly or wrongly that was what they all between them decided was the best thing to do.

But now the choice was no longer *when* she should tell them but whether when she did, she should do it alone or with Tom. It would certainly be easier to have someone to share it with, to have Tom beside her carrying their suitcase, playing his little tricks, helping to divert their minds from what could otherwise be a dreadfully solemn business. But whether or not it would be easier wasn't quite the point. What mattered was making what was the right decision from Dessy and Thady's point of view. How were they going to take it? What were they going to think of her – a mother – who took their father away from them and replaced him with someone else? Would they ever forgive her? And how could she explain why she was doing it? Well, she could give them a lot of reasons: that it was to give them a proper home instead of having to live in a hotel; that she'd be able to be with them, doing all the things most mothers did: cooking their meals, mending their clothes, being there when they came home from school with a nice fire going and a proper tea on the table for them. Which was what she was going to do just as soon as she and Tom could get married and find a proper place in which to live. Poor little mites. All those years of living in Belmont Hotel after Sam had lost all their money.

Tom was quite right: it was just about the worst atmosphere in which to bring up two little boys. It had shut them off from the real world and stopped them mixing with others of like age and making friends. Given them a totally wrong idea of what life was really like. Of course they'd much preferred being in Liverpool with Ma and Pa – and, if the truth be admitted, would have been happy spending the rest of their childhood up there. Yes, but that wasn't right either. Garmoyle Road was, as Tom kept pointing out, hardly the right sort of background to equip them for the life which lay ahead of them; a background she'd known as a Lancashire ticket collector's daughter but had long since left behind. They didn't speak that way and with a father who, even if he didn't put it to much use, had a brilliant brain, they must have inherited capacities which gave them chances of success in life unimaginable in Wavertree.

She had been a bad mother. She could excuse herself as much as she liked that she'd had to go out to work to pay the bills – and she'd had to – but they'd all of them, Joseph, Sam's best friend, and his sister, Hetty, and Tom himself, been justified in what they'd said to her at one time or another. She'd enjoyed it; not just the freedom from money worries but almost as much the freedom to spend her days doing what *she* wanted to do; and she'd been proud of her success and basked in the notoriety it had brought her. *And* the independence. She thought back to last summer's Shanklin holiday when the decision for her and Sam to part had been finally taken. She had been the only girl there who didn't have to go cap in hand to her husband every time she wanted a new dress or some perfume or a pair of shoes. And it had been very pleasant and the girls had all envied her and the men had been impressed. She'd been, and felt, a rather special person. And all done from the background of scrubbing other people's doorsteps for two bob a week from the very day that she left school!

But being, as Sam had sometimes teased her, a *rara avis* was all but over now. Paquette – her successful venture into dress manufacturing – would soon be sold and once the decree absolute had come through she and Tom would marry and start creating a proper home for Dessy and Thady. Nothing splendiferous at first – Tom still had to pay off the balance of the debt divorcing his own wife had left him with. A flat most probably – for a year or two. But then they could start looking for a house in the suburbs: Finchley perhaps, or maybe south of London. Hinchley Wood or somewhere nearer to Reigate where Tom had been brought up. Maybe even in the country itself. Of course the sensible thing would have been to go on with Paquette for another year or two, hurrying that move up by building capital. But it was no good trying to persuade Tom there! He wouldn't have it. 'Sam Jordan might have been able to put up with being kept by his wife, Micky, but I just couldn't stomach it. It's not how I've been brought up – it's not how the Fenwicks are made. And anyway it'd mean another year or two with your kids growing older and still not having the sort of background they ought to have. No, sweetheart, you've got to grasp the nettle. And grasp it firmly. That's what my father used to say to me: "Grasp the nettle firmly, Tom, and you'll hardly notice the sting of it!"'

You couldn't really argue with it. She *had* been a bad mother and deprived her children of a proper background, as much because of the emancipation that working firstly as dress designer to Culverwell and then establishing Paquette had brought her as for economic reasons. But, thank heavens, it wasn't too late to make amends. And it would certainly be a relief knowing she wouldn't have to catch that damn nineteen bus every morning and then have to stand around all the hours God sent giving herself bunions and putting up with customers' complaints!

None of these thoughts were new – she had been over them a hundred times through the long weeks and the endless meetings with solicitors as the divorce proceedings ground slowly on. But until this morning, with Ma and Pa sworn to secrecy, she'd had to take no action. Now the respite was over. Dessy and Thady were on their way now – must have left Liverpool an hour, two hours ago. Two poor little mites who had yet to learn that they were going to lose their father and that within a few months their mother would have a different name from theirs.

So what do I do? Agree or not agree to Tom being with me while I tell them?

She strove to clear her mind of temptation, to stand outside herself and see things only from her childrens' point of view. That, after all, she told herself, was what mattered – that she should handle this . . . this changeover – what an awful word – handle this changeover in such a way that they would be hurt as little as possible. To come out with it baldly that she and Tom were going to marry – wouldn't that be too brutal? Wouldn't it be kinder to let things drift on, equivocate, tell half truths and let them discover it only gradually? She shook her head. No. Tom wouldn't have that either! 'They have to be told now. You can't put it off for one day longer!' He was probably right. But if they had to be told, would it be a better thing, or a worse thing, for the man who was going to take their father's place to be there when they were?

She stared at the telephone mouthpiece, hopelessly unsure, marvelling at his patience in giving her so long to answer him.

"Oh, Tom!" she cried. "I feel so miserable about it and I honestly don't know what is the right thing to do."

He was strong and wonderfully decisive. "Micky, dearest, that's why I'm coming with you. To share your burden. You've had to spend far too much of your life having to make the decisions. From now on it isn't going to be like that. I'm going to be there beside you. Always. And beside Desmond and Thady too. Advising them, helping them when I can, trying to give them guidance. Trying to be the father they've always lacked."

It was very comforting – and what a joy it was at last to have someone making the decisions.

2

With their grandfather, a popular ticket collector at Edge Hill Station, Liverpool, having always been able to organise it, up till now, whenever Desmond and Thady travelled between London and Liverpool it had been in the safety of a guard's van, and this was the first time they had made the journey in an ordinary carriage. So they were not, as had always previously been the case, escorted down the platform to the ticket barrier by the guard. Instead they made their own way, side by side, lugging a suitcase between them, diminutive but eager and excited and not in the least concerned lest there wouldn't be someone there to meet them.

"Where's Daddy?" Desmond asked when the hugging and kissing and the 'Hallo, Uncle Tom' were over. "Hasn't he come to meet us? I want to tell him about the man who shared the carriage with us. He said that he's got a wireless which doesn't need a cat's whisker thing and I said it won't work without one but he said his does."

"Yes, well he's quite right, of course," said Tom. "The modern ones work on a different system."

"There was a lady in the carriage," Thady said, "and she'd got some birds in a cage. Two blue ones."

"Budgies probably," Alice suggested.

"Yes, Mummy, that's what she called them. Could we have some budgies, Mummy? Mrs Latta won't mind, will she?"

Alice caught Tom's eye. He gave a little nod of approval.

"We aren't going to Belmont, dear," she said. "We're going to another hotel. One called Cranmore."

"Why aren't we going to Belmont, Mummy?"

"Because Cranmore's much nicer. You'll have a much bigger room and it's got a lovely garden."

"Well, we could have budgies there."

"I'm not sure Mr Bennion – that's the man who owns it like Mrs Latta owns Belmont – would agree to you having budgies in your room."

They were making their way amongst the press of people who had poured off the Liverpool to Euston express and giving every impression of being a normal-looking family: a pretty mother in her late twenties, dressed in the height of fashion with a close-fitting felt cloche hat hiding her hair, plucked eyebrows, long dangling earrings, ultra-high heels and a pencil-slim coat over her knee-length dress; her husband, a year or so younger perhaps, a powerfully built wavy-haired man in sports coat and flannels carrying a belted macintosh and a suitcase as if it were a featherweight and their sons, so alike and so much of the same height that they were obviously twins, dressed identically in shorts and long-sleeved shirts buttoned to the neck, school caps on their heads, exuberant, jumping up and down like puppy dogs, with a hundred stories to get off their chests and a thousand questions to ask. There were few with a love of family life whose heads didn't turn and whose eyes didn't follow with pleasure and approval their progress towards the taxi rank.

"Well, Mrs Latta wouldn't have minded," objected Thady. "Where's Daddy?"

His huge blue eyes gazed up at her in puzzlement.

She felt her heart turn over. How *did* you answer it?

"I expect he's at work, dear."

"Uncle Tom's not at work."

"No, he's on night duty."

"Over that way, Micky." Tom gestured to the taxi rank.

"Who's Micky?" Desmond asked.

"It's Uncle Tom's new name for me, Dessy."

"But he used to call you Bunty."

"Well that wasn't so much Uncle Tom as the people who lived in Belmont."

"If Cran . . . Cran . . ."

"Cranmore, dear."

"If Cranmore's so much nicer than Belmont, why don't the people in Belmont all move into it?"

"There wouldn't be room for them all, Dessy. It's much smaller."

"Has it got a tennis court, like Belmont has?"

"No, Thady. That would spoil the garden."

"If it hasn't got a tennis court, how's Uncle Tom going to play tennis?"

"We've joined a tennis club. Uncle Tom's teaching me how to play."

"What's a tennis club?"

"It's a place where people who don't live in a hotel with a tennis court go to play."

They had reached the rank. Tom opened the taxi door. "In you go, young fellers . . . No! Not in the back! See those two little seats in the front there, you pull them down. That's right. In you go, dear. Aberdeen Park, driver."

"Never 'eard of it, guv."

"It's off Highbury Grove. I'll direct you when we get there."

"Right, guv."

Tom got in and pulled the door shut behind him. He was facing Thady and Alice was facing Desmond.

"So how was Liverpool?" Tom enquired as the taxi set off on its way.

"Sorny, Uncle Tom," Thady said mysteriously.

"What's sorny?" Alice asked.

"Uncle Idris took us to the Meccano factory in Binns Road last week," Thady volunteered, not hearing this.

"Who's Uncle Idris?"

"Well," Desmond explained seriously, "he isn't really an

uncle – like Uncle Tom isn't really an uncle. He's a friend of Uncle Sidney's and he works there."

"They gave us both a box of Meccano for nothing when we went there."

"Did they really?" Tom said.

"I swapped my box with Desmond for some marbles," Thady said. "I'm not very good with Meccano, but Desmond's awfully good with it. Granny took us to Birkenhead and Wallasey last week as well, Mummy. Will we be going to Shanklin again this year?"

It was a question she had hoped they wouldn't be too quick in asking.

"Perhaps," she lied. "It's not decided yet."

"If we do, will Uncle Tom come with us like he did last year?"

"Yes, Thady. Yes, he will. If we go."

"Is Uncle Tom living in Cranmore too?"

"No, he's still in Belmont."

"Well why doesn't he move into Cranmore too, if it's so much nicer?"

"You've got to keep sitting down, Thady," Tom said, "or that seat jumps up."

Thady sat down with a thump.

"You haven't answered Thady, Mummy," Desmond complained.

"You're giving me a headache with all these questions."

"How's school been?" Tom asked helpfully.

"Desmond can do his tables up to twelve."

"No," said Tom disbelievingly.

"Yes, he can!" Thady was indignant enough to jump to his feet again, making the seat flip up.

"There! Uncle Tom told you that would happen!" Alice said.

Thady pushed the seat down and sat on it again, to keep it there more than because he needed the rest. "If you don't believe me, you can test him, Uncle Tom."

Tom did so – it seemed as good a way as any to break the threatening impasse – and Desmond made good Thady's claim multiplying twelve by nine without a moment's pause for thought.

"Well," Tom said, genuinely impressed. "I never knew any child of his age who could do that, Micky."

"Oh, he takes after Sam," she answered thoughtlessly. "He was always amazing with figures."

"If Desmond can do things like that," Tom said, "it proves it really is time he went to a decent school."

"I can do up to eight," Thady said. "And I've just started nines."

"If I went to a proper school," Desmond said, "Thady would come as well, wouldn't he, Mummy?"

"Well, I don't know, Dessy."

"If Thady doesn't come as well, then I'm not going."

This was another conversation she had had with Tom. "But you're two years older, dear," she said.

"Aunty Win's lots older than we are and she goes to the same school."

"Well, that's different."

"Why's it different?"

"Because she's a girl. And she'll be leaving soon, anyway."

"She said you used to go with her to school."

"Yes, I did."

"Was Miss Seward there when you were there, Mummy?"

"Yes. She was."

"She must be very old if she was there when you were there."

They had headed up Pentonville Road to the Angel and turned left into Upper Street. Thady, who had lost interest in arithmetic, was staring out of the window, fascinated by everything passing by.

"There's a shop there, Uncle Tom, with three balls over it!"

"That'll be a pawnbroker's."

"Like Mrs Chaddle, dear. Is she still going?"

"Mrs Chaddle doesn't have any balls like that shop has. Why does that shop have them?"

"Well it came about," Tom explained, willingly enough, "because there was a man who had three sisters and he gave each of them a purse of gold so that they could get married."

"Is that what you have to have before you get married, Mummy? A purse filled with gold? Did you have a purse filled with gold before you married Daddy?"

"No, dear," Alice said hastily. "That's just a story Uncle Tom's telling you." She searched her mind for something to fill the gap. It was obviously impossible to break the news during a taxi ride. She must have been mad to imagine she could have done. "Guess who'll be waiting for us when we get to Cranmore."

"Uncle Joseph."

"No, not Uncle Joseph."

"I don't like Uncle Joseph. He's always pinching me."

"Pinching you?" Tom was horror-struck.

"Yes, Uncle Tom. Whenever he brings us a present we always have to let him pinch us before he'll give it to us."

"Is that right, Micky?"

"Well . . . well, yes, I suppose it is. It's a sort of joke."

"Funny sort of joke."

Alice shied away from getting any more deeply involved in Thady's godfather's peculiarities. "You didn't guess who's going to be waiting for us at Cranmore, Thady," she said. "It's Nanny Dawson."

"Oh."

"But I thought you liked Nanny Dawson."

"She's all right sometimes. Is she going to live at Cranmore too?"

"Yes, Thady. She's going to look after you while Dessy's away at school."

"But I always go where Desmond goes. It's always been like that."

"I know, dear. But Desmond's a big boy now."

"So am I. I'm as big as Desmond is."

"Yes, I know you are, Thady, but Desmond's nine and Uncle Tom—"

"What's Uncle Tom got to do with it?"

"Well he knows a lot about these things."

"He doesn't know any more than Daddy does and Daddy never wanted us to go to different schools."

Abruptly Thady burst into tears.

"Oh, Thady, love. Don't cry." Alice leaned forward to comfort him.

"Micky! No!" Tom put out a hand, restraining her.

"But, Tom . . ."

"No, Micky. He's got to learn." And to Thady: "Listen to me, youngster—"

"No! I hate you! You want to send Desmond to another school and not let me go there too. I hate you! Hate you! Hate you!"

"Thady! What a nasty thing to say to Uncle Tom."

"I don't care. When Desmond and I were little . . . No, I'm not telling you."

"But Thady—"

"No, Micky. Let him be. Let him sort this out for himself. It's what he's going to have to learn to do." And to Thady, reasonably: "Thady, things don't always happen the way we want them to. But when they don't, the thing to do isn't to burst into tears. It's to be brave. To keep what's called a 'stiff upper lip'. Look at you now . . . with that lower lip all pushed out and wet. That's not how to meet problems. So stop crying and tell us what you were going to about when you and Desmond were little."

"Shan't. It's a secret anyway."

"Thady, that's not very nice." And with a troubled look at Tom, *sotto voce:* "The archery set?"

Tom shook his head. "No."

"Yes, I think I will." She reverted to a normal voice. "Thady. Uncle Tom's bought you and Dessy an archery set with a target you'll be able to use in Cranmore's garden."

"Don't want it. I want to go to school with my brother."

And he burst into tears again.

With huge relief, Tom discovered they were nearing Cranmore. "Next right, driver!" he informed him.

3

The suitcase having been taken into Cranmore's hall and Desmond and Thady handed over to Nanny Dawson's charge, Tom said: "Micky, we've got to talk this over."

Alice knew that Mrs Cooper was only pretending to be studying the bill she was holding in her hand as she exited from Mr Bennion's office.

"Well, we can't here," she said. "And Dessy and Thady will be wondering why I haven't gone upstairs with them."

"We can't just leave it in the air like this."

"Oh, dear," Alice said.

"Look. Let's just go for a walk round the block. It'll only take five minutes."

Alice dithered. It was very difficult. The solicitors had been firm. Until the decree absolute was through, under no circumstances was Alice ever to allow Tom to go up to her room and even having him sit with her in Cranmore's sitting room was something they most strongly advised against. In fact they didn't really even approve of him calling to collect her from or delivering her back to the hotel.

"Come on," he said, taking her arm.

She shook it free. "No, Tom. Not in here. Oh, all right. But we must be quick."

She clattered down the steps and waited for him to catch her up on the pavement.

"Let's cross over," she said. "It'll be quicker."

Crossing over wasn't a good idea. Aberdeen Park was a private road of keyhole shape with gates which shut off its northern side permanently from Aberdeen Road – which in turn cut across Highbury Grange where Samuel was now living in the Woodstock Hotel – and gates which, in theory – but not in practice – had to be opened to enter it from Highbury Grove and afterwards closed. Within the loop the keyhole enclosed was a church, St Saviour's, and around its margin houses of varying quality with some large enough to have been converted into small hotels such as Cranmore. Because the road was private the road surface was pot-holed and gravelly but, although torture for Alice to cross in her high heels, and at great risk of spraining her ankle, fortunately in the pleasant spring afternoon, quite dry.

Tom waited until Alice was on his inside and they had begun their perambulation before saying: "I'm afraid I wasn't much help, Micky."

"Well, Thady was being very difficult."

"The poor little beggar's so used to doing everything with his brother. That's where the problem is. What sort of bedroom have they got?"

Alice shrugged. "Oh, the usual thing. A double bed and—"

"A double bed!" He seized her arm, bringing her abruptly to a halt and turning her so that she was looking up at him. "Why on earth did you ask Bennion to give them a double bed?"

"I didn't. But you know, Tom . . ." She was frowning at his lack of imagination. "Double beds take up less room. If I'd asked for a room with single beds . . . well, I don't know if he'd have had any free. And if he had there wouldn't necessarily have been one next to Dawson."

"But, Micky, look." He ran his hand through his golden, wavy hair in puzzlement. "You can't go on forever treating these kids as if they were twins. There's two years' difference between them. The fact they're the same size and look so much alike is neither here nor there. Thady's all right – he's still got a year or two he can spare. But Desmond's nine, for heaven's sake. It's time he broke free from his brother. And it's not just a question of schooling. It's time he moved into the *real* world, met other kids, scrapped with them, measured himself up against them, started to learn what life is really all about. I know it sounds hackneyed, but there are times when one has to be cruel to be kind. They're nice kids, Micky. I'm very fond of them. But if we aren't careful, if we let them go on together, sharing a bed and all the rest of it, you know what we'll be risking, don't you? Ending up with a couple of namby-pambies!"

Alice eased herself free. "Tom," she said, "I think I should go back."

"But, Micky . . ."

"No, dearest. It's for the best, really it is. They haven't seen me in months and they're all confused."

He hesitated. There was so much he wanted to say – so much to get off his chest.

"I'll come and have dinner with you tonight, Tom. After I've put them to bed. We can talk about it then."

"You've got Dawson to put them to bed, Micky. For heaven's sake, what are you paying her for?"

"Tom," Alice said, "I've got to go back across there now and one of the first things they're going to want to know is where their father is. And I've got to tell them I'm divorcing him to marry you. God knows how I'm going to do it but somehow I've got to. And I'm glad we didn't find a way of telling them on the way here. Because it's my responsibility, not yours." She smiled ruefully into his worried face. "Are you sure you're doing the right thing? Marrying me? It isn't going to be easy, Tom. This morning is only one example of what lies ahead."

"Yes, I know," he replied with a little nod. "It isn't going to be easy. But I love you. I loved you from that very first moment when I came into Belmont's sitting room and saw you sitting there, flipping through that magazine. Without you, I'm nothing."

"And with me, you're suddenly going to be a father. Of someone else's children."

"I hope," Tom said gravely, "my shoulders will be broad enough."

Alice risked kissing him lightly on the cheek for all that she would have taken a small bet more than one pair of eyes were watching them from Cranmore's bedrooms.

"That's a nice little speech, Tom," she said. "Now off you go and I'll see you for dinner and tell you how it went."

4

With the decision finally taken, Alice was curiously relieved. Entering the hotel, she went directly upstairs and along the passage to find Nanny Dawson superintending the unpacking of her sons lamentably limited collection of possessions. The boys were at the window looking out into the garden which, as she had told them, was a pleasant one with a good stretch of lawn shaded on the south by trees.

"Oh, Mrs Jordan—" Dawson began – but Alice would have none of it.

"I want to talk to Dessy and Thady, Dawson," she said.

"Oh, yes," said Dawson, who was in the know. "In here?"

"No, I think it would be better in my room. If you'll finish the unpacking, I'll see you downstairs afterwards for tea." And to Desmond and Thady who had turned to take this in, "Come along with me, you two."

Their eyes expressed surprise. They were unused to being addressed in either this manner or this way. Alice waited for them in the passage and taking one of each of their hands in hers, led them down the broad staircase to her own room on the floor below, determinedly keeping up a flow of conversation – fearful that if she allowed a silence to intervene, she would lose the momentum so hardly gained, yet still uncertain how to begin.

But it was shaped for her. As they entered her room, Desmond took in at a glance the single bed with which it was furnished.

"You've only got a small bed, Mummy! Where's Daddy going to sleep?"

It was as if the ice which hid the water of a crystal pool had been smashed and of a sudden Alice was able to see clear down into its depths. Still holding one child in either hand, she looked Desmond in the eyes.

"Daddy isn't going to live with us any more, Dessy," she said.

"Why not?" He asked it without hesitation or any sign of concern but as a practical question to which he expected a practical answer.

"Because Daddy wants to go on living in a hotel and I want you to have a proper home."

"This is a hotel."

"Yes, I know, dear, but we're only going to stay here for a little while."

"And then where are we going?"

"Well, we haven't quite decided yet. Uncle Tom—"

"What's Uncle Tom to do with it?" This was from Thady.

Alice looked into his huge, unwinking, indignant eyes and realised what he was thinking. My God, how Tom and I between us have mishandled this, she reproached herself. As if it isn't enough to lose a father without being told you're going to lose your brother too!

She cast around for some way to heal, or at least patch up the situation and hit on one. Tom wouldn't be pleased but that couldn't be helped.

"Thady," she said. "You're worried about not going to the same school as Dessy, aren't you?"

Huge tears welled as if by magic in the enormous clear blue eyes. Thady was so choked with emotion as to be unable to speak. Alice could even see his throat working as he struggled to get out the words.

"Well, you don't have to worry about that, Thady," she said swiftly. "I shall be seeing Uncle Tom this evening and I'll talk to him about it then. And I know it will be all right because we've already spoken to the headmaster about the possibility." In fact this was true. Doctor Gifford had been only too anxious to take both the Jordan boys. Findern Lodge had too many empty places. "Now," Alice hurried on. "I want you both to sit down and . . ." she realised there was only one chair between the two of them. "Sit on the edge of the bed." She released their hands and watched them as they did so, sitting side by side and both adopting an identical posture with their hands on their bare knees, their heads lifted up, their mouths open in puzzlement and surprise. A single tear escaping from one of Thady's eyes rolled down his cheek. She fetched the chair, of gold Lloyd Loom, and placed it near enough to be able to reach out and touch them.

"Now this isn't easy to tell you," she began, "and so I don't want you to interrupt me with any questions until I've finished. Right?" She nodded her head at them and both, almost in unison, nodded back, Thady energetically enough to shake off his tear and splash it on his hand which, reaching down, he wiped dry on his sock.

"Daddy and I are getting unmarried and then after a little while Uncle Tom is going to marry me instead. Until he does I shall be going on living here and so will both of you in the holidays. In term time you'll both be going to a new school called Findern Lodge which is what's known as a boarding school—"

"I know what a boarding school is," said Desmond. "You sleep with other boys in dormitories. It's all in *The Magnet*."

"That's right," said Alice gratefully. "Well, that's where you'll be going at the end of the Easter holidays." And, firmly, "Both of you."

"That's not what Uncle Tom said," Thady pointed out sulkily.

"I know it's not what Uncle Tom said, Thady, but I don't think he realised how much you'd miss being with Dessy. Now don't worry." She leaned forward and put her hand on his and patted it once or twice. "You'll both be going there together. In the meantime we'll be living here at Cranmore while—"

She broke off to collect her thoughts. It was so difficult. You couldn't start explaining to children of their age the complications of getting a divorce and how careful you had to be not to do anything which might have the courts stop it going through.

"While what, Mummy?" Thady asked.

"While Uncle Tom and I are looking for somewhere proper to live." And quickly, before he could comment on that, "And I shan't be working any more so as to be able to look after you and be at home whenever you are."

"Can we have a dog?" Desmond asked. "When we've got a proper home?"

"Yes, of course you can, Dessy," said Alice, who would happily have agreed to anything.

"And budgies?" Thady said.

"Yes, and budgies if you like."

She sighed mentally in huge relief. All those weeks of worrying and all that seemed important was if they could have a dog and budgies. As for losing their father, they scarcely seemed to have noticed it. Of course they'd had all these months to get accustomed to not seeing him – months filled with lies and subterfuge to keep what was happening from them. Had they been right to do so? It had seemed right at the start and once launched on the process easier to continue with it. Well, it was done now – and they didn't seem to be suffering at all!

5

In fact in the years which lay ahead, Desmond and Thady Jordan were never to be exactly clear at what point they had exchanged one father for another. Nor when the change took place did it particularly disturb them – it was the effect of the change rather than the change itself which was important.

Circumstances had thrown them far more closely together than would normally have been the case of brothers two years apart in age. Living in Belmont Hotel with getting on for two hundred residents – and it was not the sort of place to which they could relate or of which they could have become a part – had deepened a sense of union so intimate that it had never occurred to either of them to visualise life without each other's company.

It had been an existence lived under an aura of unremitting discipline in which meals were either taken under duress or in a barn of an empty dining room ahead of the massed descent, in which raised voices in a sitting room immediately attracted the attention of gimlet eyes and any excess of energy in a garden resulted in complaints which, fed through Mrs Latta, ended in either tickings-off or pleas for them to behave themselves 'or we won't be able to go on staying here!'

There had been pressure to conform to a multitude of dos and don'ts which was quite unrelieved by the company of other children with whom to play and exchange ideas – for Mrs Latta's remarkable latitude so far as the Jordan family was concerned had never been repeated. Patted idly on the head as if they were puppies by passing residents, they had never known the freedom of sloppy clothing, tousled hair and kicked-out shoes but were forever primped out like twins in sailor suits or blouses, with hair cut to a fringe and faces flannelled to a shine. They had found release from tension largely in the double bed they had always shared. Here they would say their prayers together and, wrapped in each other's arms, share the secret never to be told to anyone that one day they would find the way to interchange their heads and thus become one person.

Alice's decision to send them to live with her parents in Liverpool while the divorce proceedings were in hand had done nothing to weaken this bond. They exchanged their Belmont double bed for the double bed which Alice had once shared with Little Win (now Aunty Win) and – with nature, as if determined to maintain this bond, playing its part by stunting Desmond in his growth so that, although perfectly formed, he simply refused to grow taller than his younger brother – were accepted by an understanding mistress into the same form of the local Council School.

They found in Liverpool's district of Wavertree much that had been lacking in their lives. Sixty Garmoyle Road! What a splendid place it was, with a dumpy, huge-bosomed grandmother to hug and hug and hug you so that you felt enveloped in warm, reassuring flesh so soft you knew instinctively that however fierce the hugging you'd never meet with hardness under it; with a grandfather who could take his arm off and lay it on the bed, who when he kissed you smelt of stout and tobacco and whose moustache was made of wire; and then there was the house itself, with the cobwebby gas mantles hissing companionably and throwing their curious greenish light, the great black range with the great black kettle singing quietly to itself, the heavy curtains drawn, the tea cloth spread across the burgundy tablecloth, the thick slabs of bread and marge and damson jam; Grandpa with his piece of haddock or saveloy and black pudding managed wonderfully one-handed; Grandma, sleeves pushed up from massive forearms, pouring tea from the big, brown teapot – the special smell of it, the smoky warmth of it, the close-knit feel of it, the day-after-day sameness of it, the love in it. The knowing you were part of it – that you belonged.

And the world outside! There had been no world of which you could have been a part outside the ivy-clad brick garden walls of Belmont – only places to which you were taken for a treat or to kit you out. But what a world was Wavertree with alleyway after alleyway, cobbled, centre-guttered, hemmed in by high brick walls, some leading into each other, some curved, some straight as dies, all criss-crossing in a mysterious maze of streets of identical terraced houses, each with chimneys pouring friendly smoke into the sky and together forming a vast, unlimited, never fully explored playground whose possibilities couldn't be exhausted. Here too were wide pavements on whose slabs you chalked numbers and played hopscotch throwing stones as counters with a horde of laughing, screaming boys who poured out from everywhere and talked in an entirely different way, whose hands were dirty, whose nails were broken, whose socks were round their ankles, whose knees were scarred, whose shirts were torn or cobbled up, who knew a freedom you could never have known even existed in Belmont.

Here too were marvellous things to do and see. You could go to the muddy Mersey and collect crabs by the bucketful, learn how to walk on the stilts Uncle Sid had made for the two of you, go with Granny to buy eccles cakes from the Co-op where she got her 'divvy'. After the fourpenny cinema (twopence for you and sometimes nothing if you slipped in by the exit door when the commissionaire wasn't looking) there was sometimes fish and chips washed down with fizzy lemonade – and was there anything more wonderful in the world than fish and chips washed down with fizzy lemonade?

And then between Garmoyle Road and the Mystery was a high embankment which carried trains at rooftop height. Passenger trains hauled by giant locos in the maroon red livery of the London, Midland and Scottish Railway, which whistled triumphantly through the night, still gathering speed on their dash for London with fireman and driver brief silhouettes against the blazing inferno of their coal-lit cabin, white smoke pluming exuberantly behind and coaches a comet of glittering lights! Or the goods trains hauled by stubby black locomotives, often two in tandem, hauling all manner of wagons up to a hundred at a time: long flat wagons, boxed-in wagons, wagons piled high with coal – and at the end a guard's van with a guard in it who Grandpa knew, because he knew them all, every guard, because he worked on the railway collecting tickets at Edge Hill Station, because that was the job they'd given him when he had lost his arm – working on the railway.

Yes, there was much for Desmond and Thady to remember about what had been the happiest days of their childhood – those months spent together in Liverpool. Mummy had been important of course, and so had been Daddy and Uncle Tom, but you soon got used to living without them and anyway they were no more to be compared with Granny and Grandpa Lee than Belmont was to be compared with sixty Garmoyle Road.

Two

1

Although nowadays it no longer needed a degree of courage to have dinner with Tom at Belmont Hotel, when Alice entered the dining room with him she could never quite put from her mind the first time she had entered it with Sam.

She had dressed for that first meal with the care of a woman dressing for a banquet. Because Sam had lost all their money through his dealings in jute, she had parted with most of her jewellery but the first contemptuous offer for one of her model gowns, bringing with it a searing reminder of Mrs Chaddle's second-hand dress shop in Wavertree where most of her teenage clothes had been bought, had made her resolve to part with none of them. She might have the worst out of much bad accommodation in Belmont Hotel but she could, at least, be its best-dressed woman!

Occupying a bedroom in one of the terraced houses largely kept for hotel skivvies, they had had to enter from outside, pass through Mrs Latta's cubby-hole where the keys were kept, go by the hotel's sitting room and along a shadowy passage to a door which, when pushed open, cruelly, unexpectedly exposed them, standing as it were on a dais above steps which equalled some quirk in levels.

She had never forgotten that moment. Conversations in the dining room abruptly ceased. Widows, widowers, spinsters, bachelors and married couples; locals, foreigners, young, middle-aged and old; the whole bizarre collection of an hotel of more than one hundred bedrooms which catered for the sweep between the not quite destitute and the not quite well-to-do paused, weighed up and judged its new companions – an eager, spare, wild-haired man of thirty-six and his lovely, startled, fox-furred wife in her earliest twenties. It had been a terrifying moment.

Well, it was different now. From being the poor relation in Belmont Hotel she had, largely through her own attractiveness and personality, developed into being regarded by many as its belle and then later added to this accolade by – at a time when for a young married woman even to go out to work at all was very rare – astonishing all and sundry by establishing her own gown manufacturing business and making a huge success of it. In the whole of Belmont there had been no one, man or woman, who stood out from the rest as had Alice Jordan, indeed so much so that when her husband conceived his bizarre liking for a man many years his junior and invited him to join them at their dinner table, this strange *ménage à trois* had been accepted by at least the majority of those of about her age without destroying her popularity or prestige.

However, bringing divorce proceedings against a husband known not to have been guilty of the infidelity on which the proceedings (with his agreement) were being based – a man who, in spite of being regarded to some degree as an oddity, had been in his own way as much liked as Alice had been herself, particularly so by the older residents – bringing these proceedings had very much dented the esteem in which she had been held. And, having moved from Belmont to Cranmore, Alice had resolved never to enter Belmont's doors again and it had needed all her future husband's persuasive powers to induce her to do so. But having as it were bitten the bullet and faced her mainly silent critics in the eye, Alice no longer raised objections. It was near, convenient and light on Tom's pocket and with her solicitors' constant warnings in her ears it seemed as sensible place as any at which to meet. Not for a moment while she was in the hotel did she allow the situation to occur that she and Tom would ever be on their own; in the dining room for dinner and in the sitting room for coffee afterwards there were always only too many men and women interested in their presence, useful witnesses to call upon to confirm that nothing ever occurred between the two of them to which any court could take exception.

The format they invariably adopted was for Tom to wait for her in the residents' sitting room and, as soon as she arrived, to rise and accompany her into dinner. She would nod to or exchange brief words of greeting with such residents as were in the room and still happy to acknowledge her, but that was the end of it. The life she had shared there fully with Samuel Jordan was over; the life she was to share fully with Tom Fenwick shortly to begin. The men and women who had been her companions through much of the hectic twenties were part of an era passed beyond return.

And so that evening, as she sat into the chair Tom courteously pulled back a little for her, she went through the second format of glancing around the long narrowish finger of a dining room as if casually interested in its other occupants, returned nods and smiles, and then gave obvious concentration to her host.

"Have Desmond and Thady settled in all right?" he asked.

"Yes, Tom," she said, "they have. And I've told them what is happening."

He leaned towards her, enthusiasm in his eyes – but also anxiety. "And how did they take it?"

"Well it was quite extraordinary. It didn't seem to bother them at all."

He nodded wisely. "Makes sense."

"How d'you mean, Tom?"

"Look," he said. "Let's be honest. He's never really been a father to them, has he? Never played games with them.

Never shared their interests. Since someone invented contract bridge, it's been his life. That's why he's insisted on living in a hotel instead of giving his children a proper home – so long as he could pack up working for Mott early enough to get back to Belmont in time for a couple of hours of it in that smoky card-room before dinner and play till bedtime afterwards, he was completely satisfied. Well, I don't have to tell you that, Micky, do I? And now it's, what – eight, nine months since they've seen him? It's not surprising, is it, that losing him as a father doesn't bother them?"

"No, I suppose not," Alice said unhappily.

"Anyway, it's done. You've told them. They've accepted it. So now it's my turn."

"Your turn?"

"To tell you something I've been keeping as a surprise." Breaking a rule he reached across the table and put his hand on her wrist. "I've organised a flat. Well, it's better than a flat! A maisonette!"

Alice felt something turn over inside herself. "But, Tom," she objected, "we agreed that we wouldn't . . . that we'd wait until the decree was absolute before we even started—"

"Yes, I know," he interrupted. "But . . . Damn!"

The expletive and the withdrawal of his hand was caused by the approach of a waitress to take their order. He picked up the typed menu irritably. "What d'you want, Micky? Do you want the soup? Brown Windsor?" And when she shook her head, to the girl: "We'll go straight on to the lamb." He turned back to Alice. "All right?" And at her nod. "We'll have the lamb, Doris. Thank you."

As soon as the girl had gone, he said, "Yes, I know, Micky, but I was talking to Mrs Latta the other day and she told me that the top two floors of one-o-three are going to be vacant in a couple of months' time and if we make our minds up quickly enough she'll keep them for us."

"One-o-three?" said Alice, disbelievingly. "You don't mean . . ." She made a movement of her hand.

"Yes," he said. "A hundred and three Highbury New Park."

"But that would be almost the same as living in Belmont."

"Dearest, of course it wouldn't. There's a house Mrs Latta doesn't yet own in between."

Alice was silenced. Even though there was no physical connection between one hundred and three and Belmont itself, the idea of moving into a house just along from the hotel was staggering. And in any case, although she'd agreed to marry Tom, she'd been anything but enthusiastic to rush into doing so. She'd looked forward to a pause in which to live without a lawsuit hanging over her, a pause in which the last doubts about marrying again could be finally laid to rest.

Evidently reading her mind, Tom said, "Micky, listen to me. You played your part. You've broken it to Desmond and Thady. Now I've got to play *my* part which is to provide them them with a proper home. According to Gibson and Weldon it'll only be a few weeks now before you get your decree nisi. As long as we toe the line the absolute will follow six weeks after that. Which takes us up to about a month before Desmond will be breaking up from his new school and Thady will be coming down again from Liverpool."

"Tom," she said hastily. "About Thady not going to Findern Lodge as well—"

But he would have none of it.

"Dearest, hear me out. Please! A month would give us time to call the banns, get married and have a few days' honeymoon before the schools break up. We could use those three weeks furnishing the place and getting it ready for your boys to live in through their summer holidays. That makes marvellous sense. You must see that. They come home, we're married, there's a home for all of us ready and waiting to begin our new life together. We must grasp the nettle, Micky. If we don't, now that they know what's happening the situation will be . . ." He shrugged his broad shoulders. "Well, you can see how difficult it will be. Me living here, the three of you in Cranmore. They won't know where they are. They'll be all mixed up."

It couldn't be denied; what Tom was saying did make sense.

He pressed the point: "Micky, we have to put them before ourselves and it's essential I start off on the right foot with them. Because we all lived here in Belmont, especially in the way we did, and because we all spent that holiday together in Shanklin and I was able to help them learn to swim and do all the other things Sam couldn't help them with because he isn't made that way, they've got used to me. Since then there's been this gap through their living up in Liverpool. We have to take care that gap doesn't widen, and widen it will if we put off getting married and go on living separate lives." Again he took the risk of seizing her hand. "Micky, it isn't for myself I'm saying this. I have waited all this time and if it was the right thing to do I could wait a little longer – although every day I have to wait is hell. It isn't even for you. It's for Desmond and Thady. We have to remove uncertainty from their lives and build on the perfectly good relationship I've always had with them before it withers on the vine of absence. Think of it. We marry. We have our honeymoon – just a few days. That's so important – until we've lived together, loved together, we won't be the complete parents they're going to need. They come home from their schools for the summer holidays and there we are, man and wife, waiting to welcome them into the first real home they've ever known."

If not entirely persuaded, Alice found it difficult to argue against. "All right, Tom," she said. "Let go my hand. Everybody's looking at us."

"You agree!" His eagerness was overwhelming.

"I said let go my hand, Tom." He did so. "I'm not sure," went on Alice, "about a hundred and three—"

"Yes, I know," he cut in. "It isn't ideal. I've promised you a house and when my promotion comes through, I'm going to keep that promise. But until then – well, it'll give us all plenty of room and it'll be convenient, handy for the Brownswood, for me going to the Eastern and for you winding up your business . . ."

He broke off as the waitress arrived with their dinner. Alice watched it served with little interest. Her head seemed as full of unanswered questions as a hive is filled with bees. So they were to put up the banns the moment the decree absolute came through and then squeeze in furnishing a two-floored flat, getting married and having a honeymoon in time to beat Dessy and Thady coming home. What sort of marriage was it to be? They'd not even discussed that yet. In a registry office presumably. Who, if anybody, was to be invited to it? Was she supposed to meet his parents first? What about Ma and Pa? What were they going to make of what was bound to look like a shotgun wedding? And then there was Sam's sister, Hetty – well, thank God she at least was out of it, miles away in Uganda! Where were they to have their honeymoon? Who was going to pay for the furnishing of one-o-three? Tom hadn't any spare money – he was still paying off his debts. Was she supposed to pay for it or were they to get it all on the never-never? Then there were the children. What about the business of her having promised Thady he could go to Findern Lodge with Dessy, and Tom obviously flat out against his doing so? And if he didn't go with Desmond what did he do? Go back to Liverpool? Or were they to find a local school for him? But that would be difficult, if they did that – one of them away at boarding school, the other at home.

She stared at the plate of meat and vegetables placed before her and knew she couldn't eat a mouthful of it.

"Tom," she said. "I'm sorry but I'm going to go back to Cranmore."

His eyes widened in alarm. "Micky! Dearest, if there's anything I've said . . ."

She shook her head. "No, Tom, it's nothing that you've said. It's just that now there's so much I've got to think about, I honestly believe if I tried to eat any of this I'd be sick. I'm going to go back to Cranmore and have a good long think and tomorrow I'll give you my answer."

"Micky, you can't mean—"

She smiled, a little wearily. "No, Tom. We're too far along the line now, aren't we? I've said I'll marry you and I will. And I dare say you're right and taking that – what did you call it? – that maisonette that Mrs Latta's offered us, is as good a stop-gap answer as any. And I suppose it does make sense getting married and getting our honeymoon over ahead of Dessy and Thady breaking up. But I just want a little time to think it over and work out all the things that have got to be dealt with and how we're going to deal with them. You're still on night duty, aren't you?" And at his nod, "Come and collect me at Cranmore at about three tomorrow?"

She rose to her feet.

"I'll see you back," he said.

She shook her head. "No, you haven't much time before leaving for the Eastern. And you can't spend all night tapping out your messages on an empty stomach." She broke a rule, kissed him lightly, squeezed his hand and said, "Don't worry, Tom. I expect we'll do it all the way that you've suggested."

"And one-o-three?" he asked eagerly.

She nodded. "Yes. Tell Mrs Latta we'll have it."

She turned and left him – with the great majority of eyes in the dining-room following her departure.

2

Much to Alice's relief Desmond and Thady, tired after their long journey, were, by the time she got back to Cranmore, asleep. She went into their bedroom and stood for a little while looking down at them, marvelling at how much like each other they were and how much of their father they had inherited. They looked so peacful, sleeping side by side, their heads all but touching, that the idea of having to split them up and give them separate beds seemed not only a sad but, as well, a brutal thing to do. But, she thought with a sigh, I suppose Tom's right. They can't go on for ever sharing a bed and I suppose now, when there's going to be so many changes anyway, may be as good a time as any to make this change as well. I suppose I'd better have a word with Mr Bennion about it tomorrow.

She went up to her own room and although it was still early took herself to bed. I must have a good think, she told herself. This is an important evening. Tomorrow Tom will collect me and we will be making decisions which are going to alter all our lives and from which there can be no retreat.

Of all the things which were worrying her, heading them was Tom's sudden wish to rush helter-skelter into their marriage. Through all her years as a thinking child and in the early days of adulthood, it had been fixed in her mind that marriage was meant to be something you thought about deeply and looked forward to humbly. It was meant to be an ambition achieved, a celebration and something you were proud to be part of. As her marriage to Sam had been.

She deliberately forced her mind to flow back to that wedding. It had been very much a home match, hers and Sam's, with no question of any of the Jordans attending it. Sam's sister Esther, Hetty, was in Picardy serving with the Red Cross; Sam's father was no longer alive; and old Mrs Jordan held the family mansion in Crogellan. The only person outside the family circle attending had been Sam's best man, his schoolfriend and later evil genius, Joseph Mott.

But if the only Jordan attending had been the groom, Alice's family, the Lees and the Barrons – Marie Lee had been a Barron before she married – had descended on sixty Garmoyle Road and the church and later the Oak, where the reception was held, like a deluge. They sailed in from Liverpool, Stockport, Manchester, Widnes and Warrington in a mass of serge and alpaca and tremendous hats, broad of speech, loud of laughter, all come to share in the joy of the stupendous match which their Alice, their quiet little Alice, would you ever, had made. There had seemed to be aunts by the dozen and cousins by the score and if there weren't as many uncles, the greater number being proliferated through the battlefields, at least there was a sprinkling.

They were, without exception, North Country folk and all pretty much of a class. Only Samuel and Joseph Mott stood apart. But, just as Alice had remarked before over the cribbage and endless cups of tea with Pa how easily Samuel got on with them, so now she remarked how Mr Mott, the strange, mysterious Mr Mott, was quite at ease and quite self-contained . . . an island, as it were, around which the waters of Aunty Flo, and Aunty Ruby and Aunty May and Uncle Albert and all the rest of them just eddied. She didn't know what to make of him. She wished she'd had the chance to meet him earlier but Samuel had refused to let her do so before the wedding although she'd asked him a dozen times at least; it was almost as if meeting him might have been the same as walking under a ladder without your fingers crossed.

"You'll see quite enough of him," he'd warned, "after we're married. It would only upset you to meet him now." Although why it should be any worse being upset before they married than after, she hadn't understood.

The first she'd seen of him had been his back beside Samuel as she'd come quaking on Pa's arm into the huge intimidating church. And they hadn't looked round, neither of them . . . all that long way down the aisle with one side full and whispering and the other eerily empty. Not that she'd thought much of Mr Mott then with her heart in her mouth and her stomach full of flutterings and her hand tucked round Pa's wooden arm. It had been funny, Pa's wooden arm, in all that fear and trembling it had been something hard and known to cling tightly to until it occurred to her that if she wasn't careful she might pull it out from the shiny holster into which it fitted at his armpit. Of course, she told herself, she couldn't – not with all those straps – but even so she could hear the clatter of it falling on the stone as it sometimes had at home when Pa had propped it carelessly. That would be terrible. And Ma would be so ashamed. But she got to the end without doing it and then she hadn't thought of it at all, only of Samuel and the quick look in his lovely eyes, strained but kindly and reassuring.

Apart from the briefest of encounters in the vestry it was only afterwards as they stood around for the photographer that she'd thought about Mr Mott. Even then she hadn't been properly introduced – and she wasn't now because Ma had got hold of Samuel and the photographer was fussing round and, suddenly, there he was, beside her.

"So," he said, without preliminaries, "you are the young woman with the courage to marry Samuel Jordan."

It had been the strangest thing for a best man to say and it brought to her mind all the things that people had said about him.

"I've heard of you," she began, "a lot . . ."

But she had got no further because Samuel was at her side as if to stop her saying more.

At the reception Mott came across at the very first moment she was on her own.

"Well, Alice," he said. "It's time we got to know each other."

"Yes, Mr Mott," she said.

"Yes, *Joseph*, please."

To her relief one of her uncles happened to join them just then. "Oh, Uncle Harry," she said. "This is Mr Mott. I mean . . . Joseph." And, knowing she'd made a mess of it, hastily:

"He's known Samuel for years and years and years. They were at school together."

"Aye," said Uncle Harry. "So I've heard. And to Mott: "How do?"

It might have been, 'How do, lad?' Or even, 'How do, Joe?' But it was neither and that summarised the whole of it. Even if much the same age, they were poles apart.

"Well," responded Mott. "And you?"

"Gradely, Mr Mott. Gradely. And all t' better for having a niece as pretty as our Alice. Luvly, isn't she? A raight picture. I allus said she were the prettiest." He tucked his arm round Alice's waist and she was grateful. She was at ease with Uncle Harry. And with Uncle Wally. And most of them really. But Mr Mott being there was taking the edge off feeling at ease. It was curious – he brought with him a sort of . . . she couldn't define it. He just didn't fit.

Here they were around her, dozens of them. Mostly stocky or big-bosomed. All decked out to the nines. Filled with warmth and . . . and no need of hope. Because their life was real. Because it was the hot smell of bacon fat in a frying pan and blue smoke at a quarter to five on a bitter winter morning in a stone-floored scullery with a big, flea-itching, long-tailed dog scratching at the yard door, ignored because there was too much going on within, too many a ganger waiting somewhere like a judge as he looked at a time clock ticking minute by minute off. Rows, things thrown, tears. Fat arms in forgiveness around skinny bodies, brown paper soaked with olive oil to keep out colds pressed under shirts . . . cold and slimy, yet crinkly crisp against the skin; warm, soap-suddy ales in mammoth jugs, tripe and onions, fish and chips and saveloys and eccles cakes. The smell of ancient newspapers, soft and damp, stored in airless cupboards, the hiss of gaslight, yellow-blue and bright, brighter a dozen times than your cold electrics, a hundred times more alive, bright and hissing, companionable. And so much more.

She looked at Joseph Mott. Like a seed which has rested through the winter in the darkness of the earth and for the first time feels the warmth of the sun upon it stirring something inside itself to life, willing it to break out of the crust enclosing it, so Alice felt as she looked at Joseph Mott. And of a sudden she saw him as a shape at the mouth of a cave in which she had spent her life, beckoning her out, tempting her away from the dull security of the people she had always known, people like these around her who were always ready equally to strike a blow or put a strong, encouraging arm around your waist.

As if he had read her thoughts, he said: "It must be strange."

"What?"

He shrugged. She looked for his Jewishness but it was barely there. Just a sallowness of the skin. She saw the rounded forehead from which the hair had already fallen back into a widow's peak, his hard brown eyes, his long pointed nose, his certain, determined chin.

"To leave all this," he said – and he moved his hand the barest trifle as if to dismiss in an instant the whole of what her life had been.

Pa was on his feet. Ma had made the best of him. The points of his moustache had been heavily waxed and twisted till the ends stood out like bodkins. His hair had been neatly cut – such scraps of it as there were nestling on his ears – and his bow-tie had been a *bar* so straight and sure it had been across the crisp white of the high collar on which his head had seemed to rest. But the beer had smudged him now. The points of his moustache remained but one stuck down and one stuck up and his collar was limp and soiled where he'd jammed his fingers in to loosen it. And his eyes were moist and sentimental.

". . . an' it's not only in trenches," he was saying. "It's here in Liverpool, in munition factories . . . aye, an' in sack factories too! Where'd our lads be, I'd like to know, 'appen there weren't enough sacks to go round?" And he eyed the assembled company down the long table ahead of him which was now a mess of soiled plates and half-finished pies and cakes, with half of the chairs pushed back making a ragged line of what had been neat and symmetrical to start with. He eyed them belligerently as if to dare any of them to deny one word of what he had said and, by inference, criticise his son-in-law's business of making sacks.

And when the silence had gone on a bit too long, he picked on one of them.

"That's raight, Percy, an't it? What I'm saying. Nobbut but sacks out there. Miles and miles 'f them. Sacks an' wire all t' way from Flanders down to t' Voges."

"Aye," agreed Percy, a cousin to Alice on her father's side, home on leave and still in khaki. "Nobbut but sacks, Uncle Dick."

"Aye," said Pa, a triumphant watery shine in his eyes. "All t' road from Flanders down t' Voges." He was rather proud of his geographical knowledge at the extent of the British line, having looked it up especially for his speech. "An' saving our lads' lives. By t' thousand. Saving your life, Percy, like as not."

"Aye," said Percy willingly, not displeased to be a hero.

"Aye," said Pa, who, to tell the truth, was rather tired of his sacks by now but quite unable to find a way to get away from them. "An'" – picking out anyone who caught his eye—" saving your Bert's life, Carrie, mebbe. An' your David's, Bessie. An' saving mine, mebbe, 'appen I 'adn't this!" He slapped his wooden arm with his good one energetically. "It's not all in bay'net charges we're goin' t' beat t'Boches. 'S everywhere!" He grew expansive, waving his good arm grandly. "By land, by sea, by air. Like at Coofly, Sat'dy. Or like fleet in Hathens—"

"What about Rumanians, Pa?" someone shouted.

"Aye," agreed Pa, quite losing the remnants of his thread. "Millions o' Roomanians in wi' us now." He hadn't the faintest idea of what a Rumanian looked like or where they came from, never having heard of the country until the papers had been full of them coming in a week or so before. Rumanians to him were just an odd job lot like Russians and all the rest. Syrians, Greeks, Turks, Hungarians, Serbs; sometimes he got muddled which side some of them were on. There were only three countries in the war, the British, the Germans and the French. "Nobbut we 'ave to 'ave 'em, tha' knows. Reckon we can lick the Boche ourseln, us an' Foche' lot . . ."

Yes, thought Alice, there was so much to remember about marrying Sam and yet what stood out as much as anything was that chance remark that Joseph Mott had made; that it must be strange for her to leave behind the background which had made her the person that she was, the young, untutored innocent who thought as all those aunts and uncles and cousins did, who spoke as they spoke, whose ambitions were much as theirs.

But now, apart from Ma and Pa – and that only because they were firmly there, a refuge for Dessy and Thady in times of trouble – apart from Ma and Pa she was as utterly divorced from them as soon she would be from Sam. She didn't speak as they spoke; that had been Sam's great achievement, to achieve a Shavian Pygmalion – and sometimes she had felt it had been the driving force behind his wanting to marry her – and rid her of her Liverpudlian accent. In a myriad of major and minor ways her way of life had changed: she dressed in a way they didn't dress, ate food which they didn't eat, went on holiday to places beyond their imagination, took taxis instead of trams, even played games they didn't play! She had achieved a personal success which far outstripped their ambitions and – this above all – she spent her life and so established her way of thinking with people whose attitudes and philosophy were poles apart.

And all this had come about because a stranger had taken

pity on a girl being chased down an alleyway in Warrington. Had Sam not been in Warrington that day, it would not have happened. And if Tom had not chosen Belmont for his 'period of retrenchment' after his divorce, what was about to happen now would not have happened. Mott had been quite right – life was very strange: unimportant happenings such as a minute's delay which brought about a chance meeting could change its course entirely.

As hers, and Dessy and Thady's, were to be now. A husband and father were to be exchanged, domesticity was to take the place of sociability, boarding schools to be introduced into her children's lives, a business to be wound up, her own hard-won freedom sacrificed. What was it that Sam had said when they had agreed to the divorce and he had advised her not to give up Paquette? 'Whoever heard of a manumitted slave volunteering for the chain-gang?'

She thrust it from her. No, she told herself; what Tom said earlier takes precedence. We have to put the children before ourselves. So many years of their lives have been spent in a totally wrong atmosphere and under totally wrong conditions. They are entitled to have what I had, what Tom had, what even Sam had, a proper home in which to develop into adulthood. And there aren't all that many years left in which they can have it and Tom is prepared, no, eager, to give it to them. I cannot refuse that to them. I must not, and I won't.

Three

1

With the exception of number one hundred and one, the redoubtable Mrs Latta owned an entire island block of massive terraced houses fronting the north-west side of Highbury New Park and, while patiently awaiting the opportunity of buying up the nagging tooth of number one hundred and one, had converted the end house, number one hundred and three, into letting flats and rooms. It was the top two floors of this daunting building which the newly-wed Tom and Alice Fenwick rented as their initial home.

With Alice having found a buyer for Paquette, they could probably have opted for something better. But the maisonette was certainly very convenient and in a district they knew well and with which they had connections. "When my promotion comes through, Micky," Tom had repeated, "that will be the time to buy our house. This'll suit us ideally for the time being. It will give us all the room we need for now and there's a whole floor for Desmond and Thady. Why, they can have a bedroom each and a playroom in between. I know they're attic rooms but they'll probably find them fascinating."

Whilst appreciating Tom's consideration of her children's interests, Alice was honest enough to admit there were other tempting reasons for continuing to live in Highbury. With the General Strike – regarded at the time by her compatriots as more of a lark than a serious political matter – almost forgotten, it was a period of comparative prosperity. The

Locarno Conference guaranteed peace in Europe, and the steady emancipation of women – of which Alice's ability to obtain a divorce on the grounds of her husband's infidelity without the additional requirements of desertion and cruelty, was an example – made for an infinitely gayer, freer society in which she was well placed to play a part.

By quitting Belmont the crowd of youngsters with whom she had spent several hectic years had been lost to her, but this was no matter for she and Tom had joined the local Brownswood Tennis Club which offered a brand new selection of energetic young men in blazers and spotless flannels and their boyish-looking, close-cropped female counterparts. In the months leading up to their marriage, freed from all restrictions apart from those dictated by her lawyers, with an adoring swain at her beck and call whose varied working hours offered unusual opportunities for doing things at times of day barred to the majority – tennis at the Brownswood, punting at Maidenhead, picnics at Kenwood or Hampstead Heath; with theatres, restaurants and the seasonal social functions such as Wimbledon and Henley all within her financial means and, with Desmond and Thady living elsewhere, no necessity to organise her life around meal times for husband or children; with Paquette no longer a brutal taskmaster, these had been, in their way, quite halcyon days.

Meanwhile Thady had not after all joined Desmond at Findern Lodge. On this Tom had been surprisingly obdurate.

"It's not *just* a question of responsibility, Micky," he had told her earnestly, "but one of ordinary day-to-day practicality. I'm stepping into Sam Jordan's shoes and there can't be any half measures about that. Whenever they're at home I won't be seeing them now and again as I do now, but for breakfast, lunch, tea and supper. For how many years? Ten? Fifteen? Twenty? Who knows? The only way it can work is for them to see me as their father. To realise that in extremis, when the chips are down, in those things where the responsibility should be mine, it is what I say that they must do. A marriage in which the husband is treated by his stepsons as a sort of lodger they can disobey at will simply has no chance of succeeding. And their education is an important part of my responsibility. It is something about which I happen to know a great deal. Don't forget I'm not the only son but the youngest of a family of five of which four are boys. And I'm not prepared, Micky, to shirk that responsibility – to have it on my conscience, when they have become adults, that any inability on their part to stand on their own feet and play their proper part in life is the result of my being weak-kneed now and taking the easy course."

Alice had been sufficiently impressed by the sincerity of this disquisition to have her resolution weakened when Tom went on: "And if there is one thing I am absolutely certain of, it is that you must free Desmond from the claims which Thady continually makes upon him. He's a very sound child, with a very good brain. And I'm not saying anything against Thady, don't misunderstand me, Micky. But Desmond has reached a critical age in his development. He must be allowed to develop his potentialities *now* and not be held back by living a life bound up with a brother a full two years younger than he is."

Well, it had all seemed very sound at the time and she had had to give Tom credit for insisting on a point of view from which he could personally gain nothing. There was no question but that he was head over heels in love with her and she had to respect this determination to stand by his principles even at the risk of causing a rift between them.

And so she had given way – endured Thady's tears and her own guilt at breaking her promise. Desmond had been sent to Findern Lodge and Thady had gone back to his grandparents and his school in Liverpool.

2

Except for a two-storied extension on the flank of one

hundred and three, Highbury New Park, it was externally identical to the adjoining houses. Entering from the street between the standard ball-mounted columns and crossing the narrow strip of basically untended garden, one climbed an impressive flight of steps taking one above a basement occupied by unknown tenants into an entrance hall of imposing proportions. Directly ahead was the door to a flatlet largely contrived out of the extension in which a beautiful young actor somehow survived, calling himself Lancelot Carrington and resting far more than he worked. Next to him, facing the back, was another flatlet rented by Walter 'call me Wally' Trimble, a jolly fellow with an East End accent, a full, fat face, heavy spectacles and sparse but curly silver hair who worked for a firm of undertakers in Upper Street. Facing front were Mr and Mrs Abrahams, orthodox Jews, believed to be in fur, a melancholy-looking couple who dressed in black, and nothing but black. Aaron Abrahams was small of stature but with a fierce, thick, waist-length beard matching the colour of his clothes and huge piercing eyes behind huge spectacles and Elaine, his wife, was as round as she was tall, watchful, intimidating and with a voice like gravel.

The first floor hallway, reached via a dark, narrow staircase, was again of some consequence and off it there was a superior L-shaped flat which ran all along the front and returned over the ground floor hall and the actor's apartment. This was occupied by Mr and Mrs Warburton, retired out of India and other Colonial parts, a politically-orientated couple and great frequenters of the Athaneum Club just down and across the road. The only remaining living accomodation on this floor was a bed-sitting-room rented by a middle-aged Welsh commercial traveller named Iaan Jones whose joys in life were angling and stamp collecting. Sandwiched between Jones and the Warburtons was a long, thin bathroom with a WC which was to be shared between the Fenwick family and Jones, the bathroom of the maisonette above not having been provided by Mrs Latta with such a facility.

Then finally, approached by another dark and narrow flight of stairs, again leading into a hallway, this time of modest size, was the maisonette itself which consisted of sitting room, bedroom, kitchen and bathroom on its lower floor and the three attic rooms above.

It was against this background that Alice intended to start to make up for the inadequacy of her children's upbringing, that Tom girded himself to prove his undying love whilst shouldering the responsibility of another man's sons and that Desmond and Thady Jordan were to emerge from childhood into an entirely new and totally different way of life.

3

"Well, now, what are you two young chaps going to call me?"

"Uncle Tom, of course," said Desmond, puzzled at being asked such a pointless question. "Mummy, may I go and have a look upstairs?" They had only just arrived back after attending Findern Lodge's end-of-term prize-giving at which Desmond had won the arithmetic prize.

"After tea, dear. I've got you some eccles cakes. You like those, don't you?"

"They're all right. I prefer Kup cakes. It's Thady who really likes eccles cakes."

"I've been upstairs," said Thady, who had arrived from Liverpool on the previous day. "It's sorny good."

"That's a silly word," said Desmond. "We don't use it at the Lodge."

Bewildered by this unimaginable slight, Thady's mouth fell open. Desmond failed to notice. "Uncle Tom," he said, "can you make a wireless?"

"A wireless? No, Desmond, I don't think I could."

"But I thought that was what you did."

"He's in wireless telegraphy, Dessy," said Alice who in spite of endless discussions on the subject with Tom was equally undecided as to how to refer to their newly acquired stepfather.

"We tried to make one at the Lodge," said Desmond, unaware there was a problem. "But it didn't work."

"What did you make it out of?" Tom enquired.

"Well we had a box and some wire and we used a mincing machine for the loudspeaker. We had a song. We all used to sing it while we were making it."

"Sing it for us, Dessy."

"All right. Have mercy on the screwdriver, screwdriver, screwdriver, screwdriver . . ."

"Weren't there any other words?"

"No. Just those. It was bent – the screwdriver. We were worried it would break. We had a boy speak through a tube and charged ha'pennies for people to listen to it working."

"And you actually collected money?" Tom said, scandalised.

"Yes. Quite a bit."

"That wasn't very honest, Desmond. That's what's known as taking money under false pretences."

"Well, I don't see why. It was just like the one that had been going upstairs before it packed up. We thought perhaps ours had taken all the sound out of it."

Thady was desperately out of things and for the first time in his life jealous of his brother.

"I fell over a bench on the Mystery and an old lady gave me a tanner," he announced.

"Sixpence, dear."

"Nothing the matter with 'tanner', Micky. It's a word that's been in use for over a hundred years? What did you buy with your tanner, Thady?"

"Granny took it from me. She thought I'd taken it from her purse."

"You didn't, did you dear?"

"Micky!"

"You don't believe me either!" Thady wailed at Alice.

Tom found it distressing that he had a stepson who cried so easily but controlled himself not to show displeasure as the tears dripped from Thady's huge, round eyes on to the top of the dining table around which they were sitting.

It was a handsome table, highly polished with its top made out of a solid piece of oak supported on two massive pillars machine-carved in Jacobean style. As well as the table there was a sideboard, also in Jacobean style, two carvers and four smaller chairs with ladder backs and antique brown Pergamoid seats punched into place with round brass buttons. Apart from the dining room suite, the room, which was quite large, held an armchair and a settee and a wind-up gramophone with a horn. On the walls there were some pressed brass plates and a framed print of The Laughing Cavalier. The floor was deal boarding partially covered by a patterned carpet, with the edges it didn't cover stained. With Tom possessing no capital, Alice had bought all the furniture but with much still to be acquired the room had an empty feel to it and a tendency to echo.

"I believe you, sonny—" said Tom – then, with *sonny* seeming to strike a false note somehow, hastily corrected it to "—son".

"Stop blubbing, Thady," Desmond said. "Blubbing's bad form, Culpy says."

"Who's Culpy?" Tom asked, relieved and pleased.

"Mr Culpeper. He takes us for history and arithmetic."

"He must be very pleased at you winning the arithmetic prize," Alice said, rather unfortunately.

"I think your wireless was silly, Desmond," Thady muttered, between noisy sniffs. "You should have got our proper daddy to help you. He knows everything about wirelesses."

"No, he doesn't," Desmond corrected him. "He only knows how to work them."

"Daddy knows everything about that sort of thing. Our real daddy does. He went to university." And with remarkable intuition: "You didn't go to a university, did you, Uncle Tom?"

"He went straight from school to a place called Porthcurno to learn all about wireless telegraphy," Alice said swiftly. "He didn't have time to go to a university."

"Where did you go to school, Uncle Tom?" Desmond asked, pausing in transferring an eccles cake to his mouth.

"I'm an old Reigatian," Tom replied.

"What's an old Reigatian?"

"I'm an old boy of Reigate School. Just as you'll be an old boy of Findern Lodge one day."

Alice understood Tom's problem because Tom had explained. His three brothers had all been to a public school but he had been born many years after the youngest of them, an autumn crocus, unwished for and unwelcome, and the local grammar school had been considered adequate. He had, she had realised, never forgiven his father, nor for that matter his brothers, and had never managed to make the mental adjustment to having been given, as he saw it, a lesser education. He thought public school, he believed public school and without telling outright lies did his best to convey he had been to one.

"Your mother and I, Desmond," Tom went on, as if this was something which had been thrashed out at length but in fact except in the vaguest terms had hardly been discussed at all, "have decided it is time to put you and Thady down for your public school. We haven't settled on one for certain yet, but most likely it will be Marlborough." He could have said Zanzibar for all that the name meant to any of them. "The normal thing," he went on breezily, "is to attend what is known as a preparatory school first. Most schools of the quality of Marlborough have their own prep school which their future pupils mostly go to. It hasn't been possible in your case for obvious reasons but fortunately there are alternatives."

Alice saw what he was up to: he was about to tell Desmond

of St Olive's – one of several private schools on which they had obtained literature when Tom had decided that Findern Lodge had not been the wisest of choices. What she was unprepared for was the sudden volte face, so far as Thady was concerned, about to be unleashed on her.

"The Lodge is a prep school," Desmond said. "It says so on the notepaper."

Tom hesitated, then realised there was nothing to be gained by denigrating the school he had personally chosen in the first place.

"Yes, Desmond, it is," he agreed. "But on reflection I have come to the conclusion . . ." Failure to bracket Alice with the disclosure was intentional. It was, he felt, a good moment to take a first step in underlining his personal authority. ". . . I have come to the conclusion that its facilities, particularly its games facilities are inadequate. Games, you will find when you get to your public school, are of vital importance and something by which your peers will judge you. So you will not be going back to Findern Lodge. Instead, both you and Thady will be going to a new school which is out in the country and is called St Olive's."

"I want to go back to Granny and Grandpa," Thady said stubbornly.

"Don't you want to go to school with Dessy?" Alice said, astonished.

"No." And, suddenly, "I don't like Desmond any more."

"That's not a very nice thing to say," Tom said reasonably.

"Don't care."

Tears had started to fall again. Tom watched them running down Thady's face, pausing at his chin, then dripping down on to the polished table. In spite of very good intentions, he was beginning to be annoyed. It was difficult enough without this sulky little beggar further complicating things.

"Now listen to me, Thady," he said with weight. "Your mother and I have discussed this carefully and come to this decision. And that is all there is to it. You and Desmond will be going to this new school when the new term starts. It is called St Olive's—"

"That's a girl's name," Desmond objected. He didn't particularly like Findern Lodge but he'd settled in there and made friends.

"Don't interrupt me, Desmond, please. Little boys should be seen and not heard. Always remember that. As I was saying, it is called St Olive's. It is in the country and has excellent playing fields. You will of course be in different forms but, Desmond, I hope you will help your younger brother settle in. And stop the bigger boys bullying him." As they probably will, he mused gloomily.

"I left my wireless at the Lodge," Desmond objected.

"Well, as it doesn't work, I don't see that it matters very much. But if it's that important, I'll write to Dr Gifford and ask him to send it."

"He won't know where it is."

"Why won't he?"

"Because we hid it in the roof."

"You did?" said Tom, making no attempt to hide his delight. "Good for you, boy!"

Desmond stared hard at him, trying to make his mind up about this new father he'd had wished on him. It had registered that there was something different about this Uncle Tom and the Uncle Tom he had known in Belmont. In fact there was also a physical difference. Tom Fenwick had started to put on weight. There was an extra fullness to his cheeks which was having the effect of narrowing his eyes as if he was looking into bright sunlight; and the first suspicion of a double chin seemed to draw attention to the smallness of his mouth. But it was not this kind of change which was paramount in Desmond's thoughts – it was change of presence.

The Uncle Tom he had known before had been, as it were, *detached* from his own life and not too important in it. When he wasn't about, nothing was really changed. But now there was something about him which was vaguely threatening. Something which hadn't been in Daddy. And hadn't been in Mummy either. Something which, instinct told him, would always be there in Uncle Tom from now on. He would never, he knew quite positively, again come into a room where Uncle Tom was without feeling he'd have to be very careful. And of course Uncle Tom would always be here from now on because Mummy had changed Daddy for him and she wasn't Mrs Jordan any more but Mrs Fenwick. Which was funny because he wasn't going to be Desmond Fenwick.

"Uncle Tom," he said. "When we go to this new school, can we be called Fenwick?"

Tom, somewhat unnerved by the steady gaze directed at him, had pulled out his case and was in the process of extracting a cigarette. He made a business of snapping the case shut and tapping the end of the cigarette on the table before replying.

"No, son, that wouldn't do," he said at length, gravely, cigarette in hand. "You're a Jordan and there's no call to be ashamed of it."

"Oh, I'm not ashamed of it. It's just that I know that the other boys at the Lodge think it's funny I've got a different name from my parents, and if I'm going to a new school . . . well, couldn't I be Jordan when I'm at home and Fenwick when I'm at school?"

"And what would happen when your schoolfriends came to see you in the holidays?"

This hadn't occurred to Desmond who had never in his life had a friend come to visit him.

"You mean I can have other boys come and see me at home?" he demanded, somewhat startled by the prospect.

"Well, of course you can."

"Here?"

"I don't see where else."

"I'd like Harrington to come first. Harrington helped me make the wireless."

"Then Harrington it shall be," said Tom briskly, deciding that this was quite enough for an initial session. "Micky," he said, getting to his feet. "I think I'll take a stroll around the block while you get Desmond unpacked."

"Yes, dear," said Alice. "And while you're out, would you get some butter? I don't think what we've got will last till morning."

This was a nuisance. It had been a late tea and a glass of beer was more in Tom's mind than buying butter. He glanced ostentatiously at his watch. The watch had been Alice's wedding present and was the first wrist-watch he had ever worn. He was still not quite sure about it – it was only very recently that the wearing of wrist-watches for men had no longer been considered effeminate.

"I doubt if they'll still be open," he said.

"Oh, Wilkinsons in Highbury Barn will be. They never close till seven."

"All right," he agreed. "How much d'you want? A pound?"

His ignorance amused her. "Heavens, no. It'd never keep. Not in this warm weather. A quarter of a pound. You don't mind, do you?"

He smiled his warm engaging smile. "I'm going to have to get used to it, aren't I?" And to his stepsons, "And while I'm gone, you'll help your mother with the washing up, won't you?"

4

When he had gone, Desmond said: "Mummy?"

"Yes, dear?"

"Why did you change Daddy for Uncle Tom?"

"But you like Uncle Tom." Somehow they had to find a

way of getting rid of 'Uncle Tom' and substituting something else.

"Yes, Uncle Tom's all right. But why did you change him for Daddy? I don't know any other boy who's had his daddy changed."

"I've already told you, dear. Uncle Tom wants you to have a home like other boys. Not to live in hotels all your life. And do all the things like other boys do. Like playing games. And going to a proper school. And" – seizing on it – "having friends."

Desmond gave it serious thought.

"If it wasn't for me and Thady not living in hotels all our life, would you have married Uncle Tom?"

"No, dear," said Alice without much thought. "I don't expect I would have."

She got quickly to her feet and started to put the tea things back on the tray. She would have given a great deal for a little time on her own to sort out her thoughts.

"You can go upstairs and explore now, Dessy," she suggested. "Thady will show you where everything is."

"Uncle Tom said we were to help with the washing up."

"No, you'll only break things."

"No, I won't. I have to do washing up at school."

"And I help Granny," Thady said.

"That's different, silly."

"I'm not silly."

"Yes, you are."

"Oh, do stop it, please! You're giving me a headache."

"I want to wee wee."

"Well, I showed you where to go."

"Where *do* you go?" asked Desmond.

Alice explained, adding, "Oh, don't jump about like that, Thady! If you want to spend a penny, for heaven's sake go and spend one!"

Thady went off clattering down the stairs.

"Why don't we have one up here?" Desmond asked.

"Because they didn't put one in. And please, Dessy, no more questions. I really do have a headache. You go upstairs and explore while I do these dishes and take an aspirin."

Having carried the dishes in, Alice shut herself firmly in the kitchen, a humdrum slit of a room with a window at one end and a net curtain, clean enough but dingy through constant washing, hanging limply over the lower sash, a gas cooker, a big blue bread bin – a wedding present from the Brownswood Club – a small chipped white sink with a ribbed wooden draining board, a dustbin, and two wooden chairs. On the floor was tired brown linoleum.

Having put the glass cover over the butter dish Alice stowed it in a small cupboard let into the wall which was connected to the outside world by a tiny grille grimy with London dirt. She lit the geyser, filled the sink and, having loaded it with all the crockery it would take, started on the washing up only to be interrupted by Thady flinging open the door.

"There's someone in there!" he shouted desperately, clutching himself.

"What?" said Alice, startled.

"There's a man in the lavatory. I can see him through the glass in the door."

"Well, I don't suppose he'll be long—"

"I can't wait!"

"Why did you have to leave it so long?" She remembered the chamber pot. "Stay here!" she ordered and hurried across to the bedroom, trying to remember where she'd stowed the thing.

"I can't wait!" she heard Thady cry.

With a sudden burst of inspiration he ran out of the kitchen, up the inner stairs, into one of the attic bedrooms, flung open the window's lower sash and, standing on tiptoe, urinated on the sloping slated roof.

Desmond came in. "What are you doing there?"

"Peeing."

Fascinated, Desmond crossed the bare board floor and stood beside his brother watching the stream of urine running down into the gutter.

"That's what we used to do at the Lodge," he said approvingly. "It leaves the roof all stained." And, as an afterthought, "Jenkins could shoot it right over the edge. He could piss farther than anyone."

Thady felt happier. "I could shoot it over the edge," he suggested eagerly. "Not now because there's not much left. But next time."

"They'll see it coming down."

"Who?"

"The people below, silly."

"Don't keep calling me silly."

"Thady, where are you?" Alice's voice came floating up.

Desmond went and leant over the balustrade which protected the small top landing. Grasping it, he leaned over, kicked his feet up in the air and, suspended upside down, tried to see his mother but couldn't because the floor was in the way. "Come and see me, Mummy!" he called out.

Alice came halfway up the stairs, chamber pot in hand. "Get back, Dessy!" she shouted, petrified. "Get back at once."

Desmond reversed the process and grinned down at her. "It's all right, Mummy. At the Lodge we do it all the time."

"It's very dangerous. Suppose that handrail broke?" She felt quite sick. "Don't you dare do that again. Where's Thady?"

"Peeing out of the window."

"No, I'm not," said Thady, materialising. "I'm finished."

"That's disgusting," Alice said.

"Desmond says they do it all the time at the Lodge."

"Then it's a very good thing he's not going back there." She was nonplussed. In all the years of having her children, she had known nothing remotely approaching the last few minutes' experience. "Now, listen to me," she said. "Both of you. When you want to spend a penny, you go downstairs to the proper place."

"Suppose that man's in there?"

"What man?" said Desmond.

"I don't know. I saw him through the door. It's got funny glass in it."

"It'll be Mr Jones," Alice said. "He lives on that floor. Now listen. I'm going to leave you a pot." She remembered she had it in her hand. "This one." The stairs had a half landing and she came up the second flight and put the chamber pot on the top landing, then, changing her mind, picked it up again and took it into the attic room which faced on to Highbury New Park. This room like its fellows had bare boards and above at about dado height a steeply sloping ceiling. It was furnished with an iron bed made up with blankets and eiderdown but short of pillows. A naked bulb hung crookedly from the ceiling. The window was a dormer which had a short pair of rep curtains strung on a piece of wire. The adjacent attic room was similar but in this case the iron bed was a double and there was a white-painted chest of drawers. The third attic room, the largest – the one Thady had used to perform his functions – was littered with trunks, books, lampshades and the like.

"I'm putting the pot under the bed," Alice informed them. "But you're only to use it if you have to. And you're not to . . . to do what you just did again, Thady. It was very naughty."

"What's this room for?" Desmond asked.

"It's going to be your room."

"'S got no pillow."

"No," said Alice. "I've got to buy some more. And lots of other things we need. You can share Thady's bed tonight."

"Uncle Tom said we were to sleep in separate beds."

"Yes, I know he did. And that's what you must do from now on. But you'll have to tonight. Now I've got to go down and do the washing up and then start getting dinner ready."

"I've had my dinner," Thady said.

"No," said Alice. "You've had your lunch. That's what it's called down here."

5

"Same again?"

Tom hesitated. He really ought to be getting back.

"Come on, old boy," the other insisted. "Got to start off the way you mean to keep going, you know. Otherwise you're doomed."

"Oh, it's not that," Tom lied hastily. "It's this blasted butter."

The butter, which had been cut from a solid block, had been badly wrapped and was already soiling the brown paper bag on the bar counter beside him.

"Shove it in the ice-box soon as you get back."

Tom resisted informing his drinking companion he didn't own an ice-box. "I'll do that," he said.

"Pints then?" queried the barman of the man buying the round: a thin, well-groomed individual with plastered-down hair, wearing smart Oxford bags and a slipover jersey over a sparkling white, long-sleeved shirt.

"Pints."

The barman dispensed.

"Thanks, Ralph," Tom said. "Bung ho!" And, picking up the conversation where it had been left off, "Actually my county's Surrey."

"Good county," Ralph said fairly. "What d'you think about this talk of playing these West Indians?"

"Be a bad day for cricket if we do."

"My views precisely. Cheers!"

They toasted each other.

"Personally I doubt it if will happen," Ralph went on, shaking a head so impeccably flat and so highly brilliantined that it reflected the saloon bar lights. "The way I look at it, Tom, is this. Once you open the door it's bloody difficult closing it again. Have 'em once and you have to have 'em every year, like it or not. It's a question of keeping up standards, isn't it?"

"Right," Tom agreed.

"I mean," insisted Ralph, now fairly into his stride, "it's bad enough with all these wops and frogs and chinks we've got to put up with without importing a lot of bloody niggers."

"Who probably don't even know the rules."

"Too true, old boy. Too true. Pal of mine in the MCC who's in sugar or something was telling me the other day that last time he was out in those parts . . . Jamaica, I think it was . . . he saw a crowd of them playing using breadfruits . . . whatever breadfruits are . . . as balls."

"Breadfruit's the thing Bligh took with him on the Bounty."

"That so? Well, they had a pile of them, the bowler's end. They only played one-ended . . ."

"What about Duleepsinghi though?" put in a stranger just along the counter. "Bloody good cricketer, Duleepsinghi."

"Indian, old boy," said Ralph. "Different thing altogether. You a cricketer?"

"Played a bit at school."

"Didn't we all? Name's Howard. Ralph Howard." He stuck out a hand.

"Bob Metcalf." They shook.

"Harry, do the honours!"

"Name's Bill," the barman said succinctly.

"My shout," said Tom, for all that his glass was only half emptied. "Same again, Bill. And one there." He pointed to Metcalf's empty glass.

"Bob," Ralph said. "Meet a chum of mine. Tom Fenwick." He chuckled. "Just got spliced."

"Ought to be my round," joked Metcalf, a weedy-looking man with watery eyes who was dressed in a single-breasted three-piece suit and looked anything but a cricketer. "You're going to need every penny you can lay your hands on, Tom, you mark my words."

Tom waved thriftiness aside. He had a poor head and now with the best part of three pints inside him was more than a little fuddled.

"My shout," he repeated.

"This your local?" Metcalf asked.

"Not really." Tom lowered his voice. "Prefer the Grenadier."

"Where's that?"

"Down Green Lanes."

Metcalf shook his head. "Not my neck of the woods. Nor's this really." He took a deep swig of his beer. "Here to visit a sick aunt actually. Lives in Highbury Terrace."

Ralph, about to put his glass to his lips, put it down again quickly – quickly but unhurriedly, spilling none of it. There was a gloss, a smoothness to him, which advised you he was not the kind of man to spill a drop of anything.

"Well, there's a coincidence," he said.

"Oh?"

"'S where I live, Highbury Terrace. What's her number?"

"Six."

"She's got a poodle. Black one. Takes it into Highbury Fields."

"Don't tell me you know her!"

"Well, of course I do. Miss Gleeson. Nancy."

"Well, there's a thing!"

"You say she's sick. Sorry to hear that. Poor old Nancy. What's the trouble?"

"They think it's the kidneys."

Ralph shuddered. "Ouch!" He drew in Tom. "Ever had kidney pain?" And, when Tom shook his head, "Horrid. Just about the worst pain there is." He was back to Metcalf. "She in much pain now?"

Metcalf shook a lugubrious head. "Haven't seen her yet. Doctor's got a specialist coming in at seven thirty. Doesn't want me earlier. But maybe . . ." He glanced at his watch. "Just time for one for the road."

"No, thanks," said Tom, polishing off his fourth pint. "Got to be on my way. Sorry about your aunty though." He picked up the brown paper bag.

"But I insist, old man."

Tom hesitated, butter in hand.

"Have a short," Metcalf suggested. "A chaser."

"Good idea," said Ralph.

"All right," Tom agreed, his voice a trifle slurred. "Small scotch." He put the butter down again.

The barman set up three small whiskies. Metcalf brought some small change from his pocket and found it insufficient. "Fiver all right?" he asked.

"If you sign it."

Metcalf nodded, reached for his inside pocket, stopped with his hand inside his jacket, his mouth falling open, consternation on his face. "Christ!" he said. "The bastard!"

"What's up, Bob?" Ralph enquired.

"Fellow bumped into me getting off the bus. Brushed me down."

"Pinched your wallet," Ralph said commiseratingly. "An old trick that. Don't worry, I'll pay for these."

"That's not the point! I've got to pay the specialist. And the doc. And get a taxi and take her to the hospital maybe. Buy her things. Whatever she needs." He hesitated. "I suppose you couldn't . . ."

The barman was waiting, listening, his expression impassive. "Three and threepence," he said.

Tom hastily dug in his pocket and brought out two half crowns.

"Thanks," the barman said, giving him the change.

Metcalf stood disconsolate.

"Don't worry, old man," Ralph said soothingly. "We'll see you through, won't we, Tom? Poor old Nancy. How much d'you reckon you need?"

"I dunno. Twenty maybe. Or twenty-five. Yes, twenty-five."

Ralph brought out a wallet of morocco leather. Looked into it. "Fifteen's the best that I can do," he said. He brought out three crisp, white five pound notes.

"But you don't know me."

"Know poor old Nancy." He turned to Tom. "Can you manage the other ten, Tom? I'll see you get it back. Tell you what – if you're worried we can go along with Bob and—"

"S alright," Tom said. "I can manage a tenner." He didn't normally carry as much, seldom even five pounds. But he'd saved for the brief honeymoon in Brighton and for once was flush. He handed over two five pound notes.

"Bloody nice of you to trust me. Perfect stranger too. What's your address?" Tom told him and Metcalf wrote it down. So did Ralph. Then Metcalf wrote an IOU and handed it to Tom.

"Here's to poor old Nancy," Ralph said, lifting his glass and downing his tot of whisky neat.

"I'll drink to that," said Tom a trifle owlishly and followed suit. "Mus' be on my way."

They didn't wait long once Tom had gone – just gave him enough time to turn into Highbury Grange then went out together. The barman, who had seen it all before, or much that was like it before, shook his head. It had never occurred to him to interfere – his business was selling drink.

"Blast!" said Tom aloud as, hurrying down Highbury Grange, he passed Woodstock Hotel (where at that moment Sam Jordan was eating a solitary dinner in a dining room about a quarter the size of Belmont's). "What the hell am I going to tell her? Poor old Micky." And then he started on himself. "One. That was all I was going to have. One pint to wet the whistle. And I end up drinking four and a whisky! With a man I've never met in my life before! You'd better face it, Tom Fenwick. You're weak as water, that's your trouble. Weak as water. Only needs someone to start talking cricket . . ." But this was too much to accept. "'S all very well but I had to get away from those two kids. Might have come out with something I shouldn't have. Not that they're not good kids, specially Desmond. C'n make something of him. Going to! Micky's going to be proud of him. Got to do something about Thady's snivelling though." He shook his head. "Hell of a time that kid'll have at school unless he pulls himself together. Be bullied from pillar to post. Had it too soft, that's the trouble. Nothing but nannies and grannies and being waited on at table."

Meanwhile the butter was dripping through the bag, threatening to fall out of it.

"Bloody butter!" Tom said.

He glanced quickly round, then threw the bag into the hedge of a small villa he was passing. Good move that, Fenwick, he told himself. Tell her they were shut and I walked all the way to Highbury Corner and then back down St Paul's Road looking for a shop that was open and there wasn't one. She'll smell the beer of course. Bound to. All right, I met . . . Who did I meet? Someone she doesn't know. Make up a name. He remembered the watery-eyed man in the Royal Oak he'd lent ten pounds to. Met Bob Metcalf. Old school chum. Hadn't seen him in years. Just happened to bump into him . . .

He came round the corner of Balfour Road keeping close under the concealing shelter of the wall – because if he had gone looking for butter in St Paul's Road he'd have had to come back home along the length of Highbury New Park – and in through the gateway and up the front steps. It was only then he remembered that the flat bell needed fixing and he'd come out without a key because until they got another cut they'd only got the one.

He withdrew to the gateway and bending back his head, shouted: "Micky! Are you there?" When there was no response, he tried again. A window in the flat below his own squeaked open and a grey-haired, beetle-browed man with a drooping moustache which reminded him of Ramsay Macdonald thrust his head out and called back: "You there! What the devil d'you think you're doing? Go away!"

"I live here."

"No you don't. Never seen you in my life."

"I live in the flat above you!" He pointed. "Moved in yesterday."

The beetle-browed man turned away, evidently to speak to someone inside. His head came out again.

"Those your two brats keep running up and down the stairs making a din?"

"I have two stepsons, yes," said Tom with dignity.

"Well keep 'em in order!"

The window squeaked shut.

Nonplussed, Tom remained where he was long enough to see a net curtain on the ground floor flat momentarily twitch aside and the brief glint of spectacles. He remounted the steps and waited for the door to open. When after a full minute it failed to do so he seized the knocker and pounded it furiously and, when nothing happened, pounded again. By now he was red in the face and angry. Finally the door, a massive one in keeping with the building's size, swung open and he found himself confronted by a fat-faced man with horn-rimmed spectacles.

"Already got some, sorry mate," the fat-faced man greeted him cheerfully.

"Eh?" said Tom.

"Got some yesterday. A dozen of 'em."

"A dozen of what?"

"Whatever you got. Sorry."

Before he could come to terms with this, Tom found the

door shut in his face and through it he could hear the sound of retreating footsteps.

He hesitated, then began to belabour the door again. After a further pause and without warning that anyone could be near it, the door opened, but this time only by a small amount. Through the crack Tom espied a figure in slippers, pyjamas and a brilliant silk dressing gown with hair as smooth and polished as Ralph's had been, peering at him in alarm.

"'Scuse me!" Tom, with no intention of being shut out a second time, said, leaning a burly shoulder against the door and pushing it open so violently as to send the elegant figure staggering backwards. "Sorry," he apologised thickly. "Lef' my key upstairs."

At this another door opened and the fat-faced man reappeared. "From upstairs are yer?" he said. "Sorry, mate. Fought you was selling fings. We get 'em all the time. Name's Trimble. Wally Trimble. Wot's yours?" He came across with a fat hand outstretched, saying en route, "Ev'ning, Lance. You c'n go back to resting nah."

"My name is Fenwick," Tom said with considerable dignity.

The third door opened to disclose the occupier of the ground floor front, black-bearded, small and sallow.

"Party complete!" Trimble grinned. "Join us in a game 'f brag, Abe?"

Mr Abrahams withdrew, closing the door behind but leaving the odour of some strange cooking evidently going on within.

"Phew!" said Trimble. "Wonder what it is this time. Last time it was fartichokes. Fenwick, you said?" Tom found his hand encased as in a sponge. "What's the first bit?"

"Tom."

"Wally. And this 'ere is Lance. Come on, Lance. Take a bow. Probably the only one you'll get all week."

"That's not very kind," said the actor. "How do you do? My name is Lancelot Carrington." He held out a delicate hand. To his distaste, Tom noted that he smelt of some kind of lotion like a woman. And to *his* distaste, Lancelot noted that Tom smelt of beer.

Wally noted the smell of beer too. "Glad to meetyer, Tom," he said. "Come in an' 'ave a quick one. You too, Lancy. T'ain't ev'ry day we meet new neighbours."

Surprisingly, Lancelot agreed. "That's very kind of you, Trimble." He held up a long finger with a beautifully manicured nail. "But I warn you, I can't stay long."

"Got to be on stage, eh? Yeh, I know. 'S an 'ard life you fellers 'ave. Always being som'fing wot you ain't." He sounded genuinely sympathetic.

"It's very kind of you," Tom said very carefully. "But I really must go straight up. My wife is cooking dinner . . ."

"Should 'ave thought 'f that before, matey."

"What exactly do you mean by that?"

"Well anyone c'n see yer bin on a binge."

"I have not been on a binge. It is true I have had a beer or two . . ."

"Or three or four. Or five or six. An' some 'ard stuff too, I wouldn't be surprised. And what's all that dahn yer plussers?"

Tom looked – and saw his plus fours were all stained with butter. "Good God!" he said. And, without further resistance, followed Lancelot and Wally into the latter's flat.

6

Alice with her hands full in the kitchen had heard the banging faintly but not connected it with herself. She was, ambitiously, attempting to cook a roast joint, vegetables and a creamed rice pudding while in the bathroom, in the bath, one at either end, she had Desmond and Thady.

It had been a long-standing resolution that on their first

evening as a family she would cook a splendid dinner – but the attic rooms had been thick with the dust of months of unuse and half an hour of crawling around in them on hands and knees had converted the boys into chimney sweeps. She might have put them in the bath and left them to their own devices but the geyser, easily within reach, green with verdigris, explosive with power, was far too dangerous an object to tempt them with.

"Now stay there both of you a minute!" she ordered them. "And don't touch that geyser!" And with this she hurried out, leaving the bathroom door open, to go into the kitchen to check on progress.

Times without number she had watched her mother cooking a meal for a family of seven – or sometimes more when aunts and uncles she hadn't seen for years or cousins who had vanished into oblivion, were visiting – and there hadn't seemed to be a problem in the business. Of course it was only on a rare high day or holiday Mother (only seldom now did she think of her as 'Ma') had roasted a joint – joints were expensive – but no matter, the thing was she'd managed to dovetail the various components of the meal so that they all came out of the kitchen ready to eat together. How on earth was such a miracle achieved? Or rather – as Alice was far too sensible a woman to be persuaded this was a difficult thing to accomplish since it was being accomplished at this very moment by millions of women all over the country with, on average, certainly no more and probably less intelligence than she had – how did she achieve it?

Potatoes? Baked potatoes? Should she have parboiled them before she put them round the joint? I mean, she said to herself, it would have to be quite a coincidence for them to take exactly the same time as the meat to cook! And then the peas. They couldn't take long to cook, little things like that. So when did you put *them* on? Anyway, where was Tom? Must be at least an hour since he'd gone out.

Something hadn't happened to him, had it? He hadn't had an accident?

"Yes, Dessy!" she called. "Just coming!" The rice. You boiled it first, didn't you? And then you added butter and put it in the oven. But that bit of butter left was going rancid. Oh, where *was* Tom? He should have been back with it at least an hour ago! They'd just have to get one those electric ice-boxes. It meant drawing out more still from the Post Office and she'd drawn out three times in the week already. And there was still so much they needed: sheets, blankets, pillows, crockery, cutlery, carpets, chairs: there was no end to it. She hadn't even got a tureen to put the peas in! They'd have to be dished out from the saucepan! Oh, Tom, you've *got* to get that promotion soon. Maybe I shouldn't have given up Paquette just yet. Oh, but I was so tired of it. The same routine: get up, dress, nineteen bus . . . and come back after long, often frustrating and always exhausting days, far too tired to cook a meal and bath two children. And yet . . . How strange it was. Never too tired to go out dancing or to the theatre. There was that new play Noel Coward and Zena Dare were in. Everyone was raving about it. Tom wanted to go and see it. But how could they while Dessy and Thady were at home . . . Better go and see how they were getting on. No! Better turn those potatoes over first . . . "Yes, Thady, I'm just coming!" Oh, this headache. And those were the last two aspirin. Why isn't Tom back? It's only ten minutes either way.

"Mummy, are we going to have a motor car?"

"No, Dessy, I shouldn't think so. Not yet anyway."

"Why aren't we, Mummy? There's a boy at the Lodge says they've got two."

"Then they must be very rich."

"There's a lot more motor cars down here than there are in Liverpool."

"Yes, Thady, there would be."

"Why's that?"

"Because there's so many more unemployed."

"What's unemployed?"

"Not working, silly. But Uncle Tom's working, Mummy. Why hasn't he got a car?"

"I don't think he ever felt he needed one."

"Does that mean he couldn't drive it if he had one?"

"I don't know, dear."

"Didn't you ever ask him?"

"No. And now Dessy, Thady, listen to me . . . And stop splashing, Thady! You'll have water soaking through the floor and the people underneath complaining! Now, listen. About Uncle Tom. He isn't really an uncle any more. He's more like a father now because he's married to me and I'm your mummy. So we've got to think of a new name for you to call him."

"Harrington calls his daddy 'father'."

"I think that's too . . . what's called *severe*, Dessy."

"I know what severe means, Mummy."

"Oh, do you, Dessy? That's good. I was wondering . . ."

"Granny calls Grandpa 'Pa'. Could we call Uncle Tom 'Pa'?"

"No, dear, not Pa."

"Why not, Mummy?"

"Because I don't like it. And it would make him seem so old."

"How old is he?"

"Never mind that for now."

"There's a comic with this boy in it who calls his mummy 'Mom', and his daddy 'Pop'."

"I think that must be an American comic, dear. Thady, would you get out now, please."

"Why can't Desmond get out first?"

"Thady's had longer than me. He got in first."

"You had first go on the gramophone."

"Don't make such a fuss about nothing. I never heard

anything so silly. Now which of you is going to get out first?"

"He is."

"No."

"Look, I'm very tired. I've got dinner to finish cooking . . . There! I've pulled the plug out. And don't either of you dare try to put it in again."

"What'll you do if we do? We haven't got a daddy now to smack us if we're naughty."

"Dessy, how could you say such a cruel thing?"

"Why's it cruel?"

"It just is."

"Now that we haven't got a daddy, will Uncle Tom smack us if we're naughty?"

"Yes, I expect he will."

"He never has till now."

"That's because he was Uncle Tom, silly. Now he's not Uncle Tom he can smack us. It's obvious. Uncles never smack anyone."

Yes, thought Alice, that's why they're always popular. And we haven't got anywhere. And where on earth *is* Tom? He must have met someone. Maybe he met Sam! He had to go past Woodstock. That would be just the sort of thing that happened. Come straight back from our honeymoon and he bumps into Sam!

7

It was past eight o'clock when Tom came in, confronting Alice with a husband of less than one week's standing who had left smartly turned out in his brown plus fours suit with his wavy hair trim and his eyes bright and good humoured and returned (to find a wreck of an overcooked joint in a kitchen smelling of burnt rice and two fractious children only just fallen silent on the attic floor above) clambering unsteadily up the stairs, a saucerful of butter in one hand, his hair lank, his face glistening with sweat, his breath stinking of beer and whisky, his eyes glazed but determinedly jolly.

It was not the first time Alice had found herself involved with a man who had drunk more than he could handle – that would hardly have been possible living in a hotel like Belmont. But until this, her first family evening as Mrs Tom Fenwick, she had always been able to distance herself from an unpleasantness it had never crossed her mind she would ever have to cope with personally. And so far as Tom was concerned she could never even remember seeing him so much as tipsy even on special occasions such as New Year's Eve.

Shocked to the core, she stared at him in horror and disbelief as he lurched into the sitting room.

"Tom!" she cried. And again: "Tom!", the second time even more incredulously than the first.

"'S alright," he said, coming across to pat her on the shoulder with one hand while still holding the saucerful of butter in the other. "I've had all sorts of ad . . . adventures."

"You're drunk!" It was as if she was still having to convince herself that what she was saying was true.

"Not drunk. Bit tight p'raps. Met a feller." He waved his hand and discovered he still had the saucer in it. "Got some butter," he said. "Fellow downstairs gave it to me." He tipped the saucer and the butter slid off to the floor. "Damn!" he said. "Damnation!" But there was little concern in it. He stumbled to his knees and, picking the butter up, squashed it out of shape but managed to transfer most of it back on to the saucer.

"Give me that!" Alice cried out, seized by sudden, overwhelming anger. "Give me that before you drop it again!" She took the saucer from him and took it into the kitchen. She could hear him following warily. "Look!" she accused him, putting the butter beside the uncarved leg of lamb. "That's the dinner

I cooked for you! Our first evening with the children home and this is what you do!"

He had expected to face a distressed, indignant wife but he had not imagined a passion at once so fierce and so controlled. So far as it had been possible to concentrate his mind he had prepared himself to meet tears with sympathy or to stand firm against reproach. As both Ralph in the Royal Oak and Wally downstairs had pointed out, when you got married it was essential to start off the way you meant to keep going or else you'd end up being henpecked for life. It didn't matter how much a man loved his wife, he had to be master in his own house. Muddled up with this was guilt at having fallen short of the high principles he had set for himself in this his second marriage and the need to make Alice understand that he wasn't the sort of man who made a habit of coming home drunk, that this was no more than one of those things which inexplicably happened – a lapse which he fully intended to vow would never occur again.

Having geared himself to be at once masterful but penitent, dignified but companionable, loving and reassuring, he was not a little peeved at finding things were not working out in the way they should be and that all his careful planning was being set at naught. His eyes half closed indignantly. "Couldn't let the feller down, could I?" he objected somewhat belligerently. "Wouldn't have been playing the game."

"I don't know what you're talking about."

"Oh. Didn't I tell you what's happened?"

"No you did not." Each word was grimly spaced out from the next.

"Well, I met this feller. Poor devil. Aunt's got kidney trouble and some blighter lifted his wallet. Helped him out. Me and this feller, Ralph." He decided to embroider it. "Saw him home. Me and Ralph. Got his address." He fished in a pocket of his plus fours and triumphantly brandished a soiled and creased scrap of paper. "IOU ten pounds. Robert Metcalf."

Alice grabbed the piece of paper. "Who's he?"

"This feller we met."

"In a pub, I suppose!"

Tom put his shoulders back. "That's right."

"And you gave him ten pounds? Ten pounds! A man you'd never met in your life before?"

"Didn't give him. Lent him. There's his IOU."

Alice stared at him in disbelief. "And you think you're going to get your ten pounds back?"

"Naturally." He had extreme difficulty with the word. "He's a decent chap." And, cunningly, "Like the feller downstairs who gave me that." He pointed an unsteady finger at the lopsided chunk of butter. "Not top drawer, of course, but no matter. Takes all sorts to make a world." And then, irrelevantly: "*Tous ce qui est dans la fosse est pour les soldats.*"

"What are you talking about?" Alice snapped.

"*Tous ce qui . . .*" he began again.

She stamped an angry foot. "Stop it!"

"Only answering question."

"What do you think my children are going to think of you if they see you in this state?"

"Sam Jordan's kids?" It was not said quarrelsomely but as if to make sure the right children were being discussed.

"My children!" Alice flared. "My little boys."

At last, brought on by her own brave words, emotion engulfed her. She collapsed into one of the hard kitchen chairs and burst into tears.

"Poor Micky. Poor little girl."

She felt a hand pat her shoulder and smelt a waft of beer. Nothing could have brought her more quickly to self-control. "Go away!" she screamed at him. "Let me be!"

He was glad to escape from a situation he couldn't handle. "Know when I'm not wanted." And withdrawing his hand, he retreated with dignity to the safety of the bedroom.

Alice raised her head to watch him go and her anger with

herself at having given way to her emotions choked off her tears. When she heard the bedroom door close, she got to her feet and, going into the bathroom, bathed her face in cold water, then, going back to the kitchen, deliberately emptied every vestige of the meal she had prepared with loving care – joint, potatoes, peas and rice – into the dustbin, and felt better for doing so. She then made her way to the bedroom to face him and really have it out – only to find him lying on his back, mouth open, snoring. She was momentarily tempted to shake him back to consciousness but was so disgusted with the sight of him that she changed her mind, ruthlessly yanked a pillow out from under his head, collected nightdress and dressing gown and having first checked that Desmond and Thady were asleep and sharing the double bed, took herself into the other attic bedroom.

Sleep was to be an age in coming. She lay on the iron bed listening to the occasional car passing by in the street far below, with, for all the confusion in her mind, one thought so transcendent as to have her speak it aloud: "Alice, what *have* you done!? What *have* you done!?"

She was not so much asking herself what sort of man she'd married as what sort of marriage she had got herself and her children into. The shock of discovering that the husband she had expected henceforth to be master of her own and her children's fate could, by a few glasses of beer, be transformed into a fuddled simpleton capable of being duped by any passing trickster, was crucifying, yet even so was not, she realised, the main thing she had to think about. That he'd come home the worse for wear through drink on their first evening together as a family might be unforgivable, but what mattered was not *that* it had happened, but *why* it had happened – because this, she knew instinctively, had to go to the very root of their relationship.

Marriages without an occasional row would just be too good to be true and in a lifetime of average marriages, evenings which because of drink, bad temper, worry, stress, misunderstanding or whatever went wrong could be absorbed. But ours, she told herself, is *not* an average marriage. It is one complicated by the inclusion of two small boys who are sons to me and stepsons to Tom. And the irony of it is that it was really because of them that I married him!

Or was it?

The question, which seemed to have come from nowhere, rang through her head like a judge's accusation, making it impossible to lie any longer in the bed. She threw the covers aside and, careless of the dust of attic rooms unlived in for years, started to pace the uncarpeted floor.

Is that why I married him? Or was that no more than the reason I gave myself to salve my conscience because I liked what the future seemed to hold: the company of a man who was head over heels in love with me and was going to free me from the slavery of Paquette and actually be the family breadwinner! And sex. Didn't that come into it? Of course it did! Maybe I wasn't made like his first wife was, or like some of those girls in Belmont, girls like Dot and Poppy who seem to think of nothing else, but it was exciting being with him in a way it had never been exciting with any man before, feeling his arms about me, the enormous strength in them, his masculinity. Until Tom came along it had always seemed to me that sex was a grossly exaggerated business – but with Tom I wasn't so sure. Couldn't help wondering, hoping even, he'd light the spark in me no one had till then. So why didn't I let him have sex with me *ahead* of our getting married? Because I didn't want to risk getting pregnant? Because I didn't want to cheapen our relationship? Because I'd feel disloyal to Dessy and Thady? Excuses. Nothing but excuses! The real reason was that I didn't want to risk finding out that having sex with him was no different from how it had been having sex with Sam!

Which means? That I was frightened of admitting to myself that my reservations about marrying him were justified. That

I wanted to stifle my own doubts. It was as if I'd got myself involved in a progression there was no way of stopping. I knew I didn't love him but it seemed – well, almost too much of an effort to stop the thing in its tracks. Like I'd climbed aboard a juggernaut which was gathering speed with, at the bottom of the hill, the registry office! Whenever the doubts arose I either buried my head in the sand or told myself it was the right thing to do for the children's sake! And the one thing I religiously refused to do was look ahead and analyse in depth what foisting another father's children on a man like Tom could lead to.

She felt the sudden sharp pain of a splinter driven into her foot. She winced but made no sound, hopped across the room, found the switch and sitting on the bed examined her foot in the cold hard light of the unshaded bulb. The splinter was easy to find, projecting at least a quarter of an inch from the flesh. She gripped it with her fingernails and pulled it out and watched the red blood mingle with the thick grey dust layer on her skin. How easy it is, she thought. You do something silly like walking in bare feet on a wooden floor and pay the penalty. But a quick wrench and then wash your feet and maybe put a bit of iodine on and it's all over. But you can't do that for a marriage. And if this one's going to be as wrong as all my instincts are now warning me, well, unless I'm going to leave this husband too – which is surely unimaginable – then I'm going to have to pay for it, for the rest of my life maybe. And what's worse, far worse, is that Dessy and Thady are going to have to pay for it as well and until they grow up there's nothing they can do about it. Why didn't I work it out? Why didn't I face up before it was too late to the problems that were bound to arise in trying to thread a path between their wants and Tom's wants which would somehow leave none of them feeling neglected? And then the business of their different make-ups! On the one hand two boys who'd never shown the slightest interest in games and on the other a stepfather who thinks of precious little else!

And now I've discovered it's not even as simple as that! Half an hour across a tea table has shown me that I didn't even know my *children's* make-ups! Listening to them was like listening to strangers! They spoke and behaved in ways I simply couldn't have imagined. All right! Maybe that was because they were under stresses they'd never had to endure before, but that doesn't help. Because those stresses aren't going to go away; they're going to be even greater when Tom isn't so willing to make the effort and Dessy and Thady start seeing him as a tyrant insisting they behave in ways they feel he has no right to. It's one thing a husband and wife standing shoulder to shoulder facing the most intractable problems with children they've created; but if a mother sides with a stepfather the children will be jealous and bitter and if she sides with the children, then the husband will be.

And what about Tom getting drunk anyway? She'd known him for what? Nearly two years. And in all that time his behaviour towards her had been exemplary. Of course, with Belmont not having a licence the likelihood of him being tempted to drink more than he could handle was obviously reduced. And if – as presumably must have happened sometimes, as for example in evenings spent with his rugger friends after an unexpected victory – he *had* drunk a bit too much, he must have been scrupulously careful not to let her see how it affected him. Yet an hour's embarrassment of having to handle two small boys for whom he was now responsible had sent him to a pub to return to her a sozzled wreck!

Why?

Because, however brave on a rugger pitch, however highly principled and well meaning, Tom was proved basically weak. Unable to cope with the stepsons he'd inherited, he'd escaped to the reassurance and security of a pub and the company of men with whom he felt he *could* cope. And faced with similar pressures in the future it would happen again. The man was terrifyingly flawed!

It was a devastating discovery – but she knew without the slightest doubt that her reading of him was correct.

And it was not the only discovery of this cataclysmic day. There was something even worse: the totally unimaginable discord between Dessy and Thady. No two brothers could have been as close as they had been. They had wanted no one else for company – until this afternoon she could not recall so much as a cross word between them. Their lives had been totally bound up in each other, they had felt no want of friends or of companionship. And now here was Dessy clearly regarding his younger brother as a nincompoop and Thady desperately distressed at suddenly finding himself rejected. And hers the fault again because she had yielded to Tom's insistence and allowed them to be brutally wrenched apart on the altar of growing up.

Sick at heart she went to the attic window and leaning her elbows on its narrow sill and supporting her chin on her hands stared out into the night. She couldn't see the street below because the slated roof cut if off from vision – all she could see was the rooftops and upper floors of the houses opposite and one or two of the street lights stretching along towards Highbury Quadrant at the end. There were no motors now; it was far too late for the few which used Highbury New Park. The whole world seemed dead and silent – as bereft of purpose as she felt herself.

She pulled herself together. Partly through bad luck, but probably even more through selfishness on her own part, she'd made a mess of her children's lives thus far. But the one thing she was not, and would not be, was bereft of purpose. I have a very *real* purpose, she told herself: to find the best answer for them for the future. From now on everything has to be directed to that end. And it will be. That doesn't mean that I'm to get nothing out of life, I'm not a nun entering a monastery; it doesn't even mean that Tom and I can't share a way of life together – but what it does mean is that whenever

I have to make the important decisions Dessy and Thady must come first.

This decision brought Alice comfort and she turned out the light, went back to the iron bed and after a while fell into a fitful sleep.

Four

1

The following morning when, with eyes which felt like holes, Alice went down at dawn to face the day ahead, she found a note awaiting her. It was in an envelope with 'Micky' written across it in Tom's clear, almost copperplate, handwriting.

> *Micky, I won't try to make love to you in this. I know you must almost hate me today and I loathe myself for hurting you so much. I cannot face you yet. I am too ashamed. But whatever you may think, I love you more than anything in the world and I always shall. What happened last night is a weakness in me but I will fight it down and I give you my solemn word of honour you will never have to put up with it again. My dear, I beg you to forgive me and to give me a little help. You see, you are everything to me and I am really in great need of you in this thing. I can't write any more, Micky, I am too fed up with myself. I will come back this evening, after you have put the children to bed. Please believe me. I will do all I can to atone for the wrong that I have done to you. All my love, Tom.*

She stared at the words in horror. Was this the man she had divorced Sam for? This weak, snivelling apologist? And what did it mean? *What happened last night is a weakness in me . . . I will fight it down . . . I am really in great need of you in this thing.* Surely it could not mean what it seemed to mean. That this had happened before! That this perhaps was the real reason why his first wife had divorced him! That the story that she was . . . what was the word? . . . a *nymphomaniac* . . . was just a cover-up excuse?

She closed her palm on the letter, scrunching it to a ball, and stood looking around the room: at the Jacobean dining suite, the chairs, the curtains, settee, gramophone – everything paid for by herself. The beginnings of the home for Dessy and Thady. She thought of the awful room in Stradbroke Road from which the skivvies had been shifted to provide accomodation for her and Sam after they had lost their money – a room with a sagging double bed, a square of carpet frayed at its edges and diseased by threadbare patches; a room with dingy curtains over yellowing net, stained walls and everywhere the evidence of its previous occupants: soiled underwear, spilt powder on the dressing table, unwashed cups and saucers and over everything an odour of damp and stale sweat and a sense of abandonment of self-respect. She thought of the room which led off it, unlit by windows and so narrow it had been dubbed thereafter the Slit, the room in which Dessy and Thady were going to have to sleep; she thought of the smirking Irish porter who had taken them over from the hotel and, while they inspected this horror of accommodation so different from the splendid house in Nether Street they had been forced to quit, had lolled against the passage wall which led to it, a wall from which half a dozen layers of paper peeled and mouldered displaying crumbling lath and plaster underneath.

Well, this at least was better. Better, yes, but wrong. Wrong because – if she was going to be honest – the reason they were here wasn't because the extra floor gave Dessy and Thady an extra room to play in but because it had suited her and Tom. They were here because it was handy to the Brownswood Club, convenient for Tom to go to work from and near enough not to lose touch with friends.

She went to the window and stared at the clouded sky. What time was it? It must still be early. What? Five perhaps? Half past? Thank God the children were still asleep. Please don't wake yet, Dessy and Thady. Please give me a little time to work this out.

What am I going to do? What am I going to do if this is to go on, if last night is to be a pattern for the future?

Another divorce? She shook her head. Another divorce was not merely unimaginable but probably inconceivable – what court would let her duck out of marriage a second time without the most damning of evidence?

Then what was she to do? How to find the way to prevent a repetition of last night's disaster? Well, he loved her; and he was at heart a decent man who wanted to give her happiness. These were strong cards in her hands – perhaps the only effective cards she had. She would have to use them. When he came back tired, ashamed, begging forgiveness, she would state her terms. This once she would excuse him – this once only. If it happened again she would leave him. Tell him there was still more than enough money in her Post Office account to see her and the children through a few months while she started another business – or went back to Culverwell who had told her that if she found housewifery too dull there would always be a job with him available. These would be strong cards; cards available to very few women. But would they be strong enough to offset the stress of continually sharing his life with Dessy and Thady? Of sharing her with them? Even as she asked herself the question, she knew that they would not. If for fifty-two weeks each year, for seven days of every week, he had to come back from work and tussle with the unending problem of bringing up another man's sons who had already shown their different attitudes and personalities, sooner or later he would break his promise.

She realised there was only one possible solution: to go along with the volte-face Tom had so surprisingly sprung on her the day before that both Dessy *and* Thady should go to a boarding school. Why he had come to this sudden conclusion, whether or not it was because at some time during that taxi ride some instinct had warned him it was the right course to take, was unimportant. What mattered was that it was an answer: by limiting the time he would have to spend with Dessy and Thady to school holidays while through term times she was entirely his, the pressure would be reduced. Wrack her brains as she might, she could think of no other answer. Perhaps if they did that it would work out. Perhaps. And if it didn't? Her mind made up, she shrugged. She would meet that situation when it arose.

2

St Olive's brought into Desmond and Thady Jordan's lives a dimension which until then they had not known existed, for it was in Wormley which, was, in the autumn of the year nineteen hundred and twenty-eight, in the country. It is true that the London bus did in fact go a little further north along the Great Cambridge Road, perhaps half a mile or so, but here there was nothing much more than a public house and an enormous gravelled turning-space so that descending Londoners arriving for the first time were conscious of a feeling of World's End *déjà vu* which was puzzling except to those who realised its similarity to the back-of-beyond outposts they had seen portrayed in American Western movies.

Apart from seeing the countryside passing by from the windows of guards' vans or, more latterly, passenger compartments, the nearest they had been to it had been in the halcyon days of their parents' prosperity when they had attended a nursery school in Barnet, a happy place with a pretty garden, run with love and affection for boarded-out children of tender age. Otherwise the world had always been limited for Desmond and Thady to endless acres of houses, large and small, all belching up smoke into a sky which returned it later as soot or dirty rain and snow, and mile upon mile of hard, unforgiving pavements, street lamps, horse, motor or hand-drawn traffic, noise, dust, fog and smell, with just here and there strange green areas known as 'parks' deserted when cold or wet, crammed full on better days.

But St Olive's, a rambling Victorian house just about large enough to call itself a mansion and possessing various outbuildings capable of being recast as classrooms, was set in twenty acres of more or less open pastureland bounded on its western flank by the placid canal-like New River while on its farther side lay a large and heavily-wooded private estate known as Pym's Park which was strictly out of bounds – through accessible to intrepid explorers by a convenient footbridge – and had a large lake of boomerang shape which was thrown open for skating to the boys of St Olive's and local villagers when it froze.

As for the school itself, for all the exciting promise a glowing brochure held out, it had little enough to recommend it, being one of the myriad of post Great War private ventures – founded by retired army officers, and largely staffed by failed schoolmasters – which catered for those with a wish to avoid the impedimenta of children for as large a proportion of the year as possible or those with a snobbish bent but unable to afford genuine preparatory and public schools.

The proprietor had been a Colonel Latham, now deceased, who had combined the doubtfully interlocking roles of owner and headmaster. On his death his widow, Rebecca Latham, seeing no reason to deprive herself of an eminently satisfactory income and way of life, had filled the gap in the establishment by elevating Mr Donleavy – until then euphemistically described as Deputy Headmaster – and promoting him with a doctorate. She had also engaged Captain Elliott, who claimed to have recently retired from the Army Educational Corps – a claim which Mrs Latham had decided it would be discourteous to check – to make the numbers up. In her brochure, Mrs Latham had perspicaciously included in Captain Elliott's duties those of 'physical training instructor and games and swimming coach' and it was this, and his army rank, which had impressed Tom Fenwick.

Since it was, as Tom had explained to Alice, too late to send Desmond to a recognised preparatory school and it would be unfair to enter Thady now, the sensible thing was to mark time and see how the boys developed before deciding which was the right public school to select for them. Meanwhile St Olive's, with its resident games master, looked to have just the right amount of weight to prepare them for the rough and tumble of their final schooling.

Most of this kind of reasoning had been impressed on Alice through the weeks leading up to their marriage and at a time when she had had no reason to doubt the judgement of a man whose education if not perhaps up to Samuel's standard had been at least as good as most of those living in Belmont and infinitely broader than her own. In any case her original qualms – now offset by the removal of pressure in her marriage if she gave way – had always been directed far more to the wisdom or otherwise of sending them to boarding school at all than to the possible shortcomings of St Olive's.

Mrs Latham proved to be a tall, gaunt woman who modelled herself on Edith Sitwell. Her hair was dressed absolutely straight to fall over her ears on either side of ashen cheeks leaving her forehead totally exposed. She would have none of modern dress but wore strange, long cloaks which swished the ground and gave warning of her coming.

She bade them all good morning and then, facing the children, took Desmond's and Thady's hands in hers and stood holding them in silence for some time as if she could read their characters through some current passing between them.

"Good. Good," she said, as if she had learnt all she required to know and found it satisfactory. She had a high-pitched, distant voice which conveyed that she lived in another world to this one and would return to it as soon as these unavoidable preliminaries were through. "You would no doubt like to see the dormitories?" She spoke without undue enthusiasm as if this extraordinary desire of parents actually to inspect the rooms in which their offspring were going to sleep still baffled her.

"Yes, please," said Alice, daunted, unfairly reading something of Hetty Jordan in her. "If it isn't too much trouble."

Mrs Latham studied her. Alice was dressed in a simple but very smartly up-to-date Oxford blue dress with the latest high-belted waist and flared cuffs, a cloche of the same material pulled down right to her eyes, silk stockings, high-heeled shoes (quite unsuitable for the occasion) and a fox fur. Never been round a school before, Mrs Latham conjectured – she shouldn't be much trouble. How about him?

She examined Tom who wore a suit and his Old Reigatian tie, observed the brilliant polish of his shoes, the meticulously clean hands and fingernails, the eagerness of his manner and, remembering the points he had touched on in an unnecessarily long correspondence, knew exactly what to say.

"It isn't a question of trouble, Mrs Fenwick," she replied rather loftily. "As I am sure your husband would be the first to confirm, one of the essentials of a quality preparatory school is that the dormitories should not only be clean and comfortable – without of course being *too* indulgent – but should be located near enough to authority to ensure that proper order can be kept." And, to a teenage boy standing discreetly at a distance, clearly under instruction: "Webster!" He came over. "This is Desmond Jordan. And this is his brother, Thaddeus. Thaddeus will be in Form One, Desmond in Two. I want you to show them their classrooms and then take them to Captain Elliott in Great Field." And without delay: "This way, Mr and Mrs Fenwick, please."

Had it not been for her loss of confidence in Tom, it is probable that by the time the tour of inspection had been completed Alice would have left St Olive's with her doubts set at rest. It was true the dormitories with their regimented beds each with a small locker beside it put her in mind of hospitals and the classrooms (of which there were four – one in a barn, one in what had once been a row of stables, one in a conservatory and one in what had once been a music room and still had a piano in it) had rather a make-do feeling to them but the dining room was impressive with school cups in their niches and boards of prize-winning pupils – a number of whom, Mrs Latham had casually mentioned, had gone on to a Varsity and were promising great things in the years ahead – and the occasional master whisking by in his gown and mortar board imparted a compellingly scholastic air.

Tom was unreservedly enthusiastic but whereas a few weeks earlier Alice would have accepted his judgement unquestioningly, now the uncertainty which accompanied her in the taxi back to Highbury arose less from faults she had found in the school itself and more from his uncritical blanket approval of St Olive's – an approval he had communicated, over-fulsomely she felt, to Mrs Latham on their departure. And his attempts to set her mind at rest, rather than allaying her doubts, merely emphasised them.

"I realise," he said in a kindly way, laying his hand on her knee, "how difficult it is for you, Micky, to make a judgement when you weren't lucky enough to have had a private education. Boarding schools are quite different animals and they have to have stricter rules and regs or all you get is anarchy. I'm not saying I don't wish Colonel Latham wasn't still alive – judging by those results he obviously knew his business. But Doctor Donleavy has got a pretty good idea of where he's going. I liked the cut of his jib and his background's excellent. Haileybury, you know – which I would have preferred for myself, but my father didn't think I was cut right for a military career." And then, seeing the contradiction this implied: "What a pity you didn't wear flatter shoes and then you could have walked over the playing fields with us. The main one, the one they call Great Field, 's got a few trees that need removing and then they'll be able to get in a second football pitch. And Elliott tells me their long term plan is for a running track all round it. Good fellow, Elliott. Played two or three times at Twickenham he tells me."

Perhaps more than this everlasting concentration on sports, to which she had anyway become accustomed, his continual use of clichés had lately begun to worry Alice – and this as much because she was aware that, although he had always larded his conversations with them, it was only since the butter incident she had been bothered by it. It was puzzling. Sam's friendship with him had initially come about because Tom was reputedly well read. But Sam had rarely needed to fall back on stereotyped expressions – had always been coming out with original, often, it was true, outlandish remarks to make his points. But through their many months of companionship Alice could not recall a single creative observation from Tom. And so the question had to be asked – why all this reading? Looking back at their earliest days of marriage she could hardly imagine Sam without a book near at hand but it had never occurred to her to ask him why he read so much or why it gave him so much pleasure and satisfaction, so why was she asking the question of Tom now? But even as she asked herself this question she knew the answer to it. Sam had read for pleasure, for discovery, for the broadening of his mind – but Tom read because reading was a substitute for living just as clichés were substitutes for inventiveness and playing games a substitute for life's reality.

Now, disturbed by his over-ready approval of everything at

St Olive's and depressed by this fresh battery of clichés, she decided that the time had come when reality must be faced.

"Tom," she said. "You've got Marlborough in mind for when they leave St Olive's, haven't you?"

"Marlborough," he agreed. "Or Haileybury perhaps."

Which said a great deal.

"You've never suggested Haileybury before."

"True. But it's been in my mind as a possibility."

"Would it make much difference – from a cost point of view, I mean?"

"Oh, no. The fees would be pretty much the same."

"And what *would* they be?"

He shrugged. Obviously he had little idea. She decided against pushing him too far into a corner.

"Well, whatever they are, could we afford them? Out of what you're getting at the moment?"

"Well, it would be a bit tight. But you don't have to worry. By the time they're ready to go, my promotion will have come through." And, giving her knee a little squeeze before removing his hand: "Now you're not to worry your pretty little head about such things. That's my job from now on. See these?"

There was such an enthusiasm in his voice that she barely glanced at the slips of paper he was holding out to her but up at him and saw that his eyes were lit with triumph.

"What have you got there, Tom?"

"Two tickets for His Majesty's tonight."

"His Majesty's! But that's the new Noel Coward thing, isn't it?"

"*This Year of Grace.*"

"But it's only just opened. How on earth did you manage to get tickets?"

He raised and wagged a finger, a broad grin on his face. "We have our little ways and means."

"Oh, Tom, how wonderful! When did you get them?"

"As soon as we heard the Manchester reviews."

"You've had them all that time? And you didn't tell me? They must have been burning holes in your pocket."

He chuckled happily. "They were."

She was almost speechless. "Oh, Tom. You're so kind to me."

"Not kind," he said. "Grateful. Grateful to you for filling the void in my empty life and making it real."

After her recent thoughts, she felt shameful. She swivelled on the taxi seat so that her knee was pressed against his thigh and her face was very close to his. She would have given the world to be able to echo his words.

"Don't say such things," she whispered, leaning to kiss him lightly on his cheek. "They embarrass me." And, after a moment, "And they ask more from me than I can ever give you."

He shook his head. "You have given me more than I deserve, more than I ever hoped from life, more than I could ever have imagined." He put his hands up to her shoulders as if to make sure she did not withdraw from him. "You cannot conceive how much I love you. There is nothing else in my life but you. All that matters is that I should be worthy of you and make you happy."

And in this for a while he succeeded. With the stress of balancing her affections between her husband and her children removed, Alice was aware of a freedom she had not imagined. The weeks, the months flew by and she was able to write to her mother:

> *No one could be more kind or thoughtful. There's hardly a day goes by when he doesn't bring me a present of some sort. Only small things of course, because until his promotion comes through, we do have to be a little careful. Most Saturdays, unless*

Tom happens to be on duty, I go to watch him playing rugger for the Exiles and afterwards a crowd of us usually go on somewhere to dance. Oh, mother, he really is quite brilliant. Pa would be so impressed if he could watch him even though it isn't the kind of rugger he used to play for Widnes before he lost his arm. Why don't you try and persuade him to come and visit us? I know how much he thought of Sam, but our marriage had to come to an end, we hadn't anything more to give each other and there were the children to consider. Now, although they are at boarding school and I miss them terribly, at least they do have a home to come back to instead of just a hotel bedroom. We've plenty of room and Tom is anxious to meet you both. And I could take you round London and show you so many exciting places now that I have the time. Oh, mother, if you knew what it was like not to have to get up in these winter mornings and catch that blessed bus and then stand on my feet all day long with those sewing machines whirring in my ears and customers grumbling at me all the time. Oh, mother, I'm so happy now . . .

* * *

Christmas brought the children home. There was a Christmas tree and a massive turkey which Alice, who had picked up domesticity with contemptuous ease, cooked and carved while Tom pulled crackers and wore a paper hat. There was a Christmas pudding studded with threepenny bits which, miraculously, only seemed to be discovered in the children's portions. There had never been a Christmas like it – not for Tom, not for Desmond and Thady, not for Alice. A quiet Christmas, true, so unlike the Christmas they would all be having just a few doors along at Belmont with the fancy-dress balls, the new styled evening dresses, softer, the waist coming down at last, hems dipping to the ankles at the back, the latest syncopation, latest dances, latest crazes, the shrieks, the gaiety, the parties, parties, parties, the final frenzy of a section of a generation which insisted that the past with its restrictions, conventions, hide-bound rules, was over and done with, forgotten, buried, that the present was here to stay, that life was jazz, cocktails, laughter, freedom, independence; a section of a generation which for all the portents refused to face reality, switched off the news, turned to the comfortable pages of the newspapers and salved consciences with coppers for ex-servicemen, medals chinking, singing from the gutter to a theatre queue.

And then it was New Year's Eve and the sounds of jollity, the feverishness, the wild abandon of Belmont's young drifted along reminding Alice of what she had given up in marrying Tom and she was without regret. She had discovered his limitations and learnt to live with them. She counted her blessings: her little boys, her considerate husband, her relative security. No more than the young of Belmont did she look ahead. In no time at all it would be spring and there would be tennis again, picnics, days on the river, and maybe even, when Tom got his promotion, a motor car!

Five

1

But when spring came, it brought disaster.

Alice heard Tom out, his tone breezily cheerful, his expression jocund – and saw through the pitiful defence of a man shocked and bewildered.

"What you're saying, dear," she insisted gently, "is that you're going to lose your job."

"Oh, no, Micky. That's quite the wrong end of the stick."

"Is it? Then explain it to me again."

He did. It seemed there was going to be a merger of the Empire's old cable and wireless interests and operating companies and that a new company, which would trade under the grandiloquent title of Imperial and International Communications Limited, was being formed which would coalesce these various separate enterprises. Vast economies in running costs would result – largely by shedding labour.

"It all makes sense," Tom concluded, as if it had been his own idea – while Alice remembered how at a dinner he had shared with herself and Sam and Tom at Belmont, Joseph Mott had, with terrifying accuracy, forecast that something like this was bound to happen.

"Sooner or later," Tom was going on as if reading her mind, "it was bound to happen." He waved a confident hand. "But to say that any of us are going to lose our jobs . . . as if we were being sacked or something . . . well, that would be absurd.

We all have contracts. Well, not the general office staff, of course . . ."

She helped him a little. "The specialist operators? Those with a Porthcurno training?" she suggested.

"Exactly. These people can't just pitch us out as if we were clerks!" There was a world of derision in the word. "If they want us to go then they have to buy us out. And so long as we stick together . . . as we will . . . we can force their hands. Bring them to heel!"

She felt for him, a man with his world crumbling around him trying to salvage self-respect; she felt for him, but would not be deflected from facing reality.

"How much are they offering you, Tom?" she asked.

"Oh," he said quickly. "It's a generous enough offer, so far as it goes." And she knew before he told her that however much he protested, this was all he'd get and he knew it too. "They're offering a lump sum of one thousand pounds and a pension of one hundred and four pounds a year for life."

One hundred and four pounds a year, she thought sadly. Why doesn't he just come out with it and say two pounds a week. It's not his fault after all. He's done nothing dishonest. He wouldn't. He couldn't – dishonesty, one had to admit, called for a degree of enterprise.

"And if you don't accept it?"

"You can do a lot with a thousand pounds, you know."

She thought of the fifty pounds borrowed from her mother, of the two hundred and fifty pounds on which she had founded Paquette.

"Yes, Tom," she agreed. "You can. It's a lot of money."

"And a pension of one hundred and four pounds a year! For life!"

Yes, she thought drily, two pounds a week – it's much more than a family on the dole gets. Four times as much. And I suppose it's about what Pa brought us all up on somehow. But she thought as well of the rent they paid, of the food they ate, of the children's school fees, of the clothes they were always needing, of the Brownswood Club, of the planned return for the third time to Shanklin in the summer, of that motor car.

"Have you thought about what you're going to do, Tom?" she asked. "After all you must have known about this for some time."

He flushed. His cheeks were fuller still, his body on hers when they made love was heavier by the day.

"As yet that doesn't arise," he said. "I have still to make my mind up."

"What happens if you don't accept the offer?"

"Well, of course I stay on."

"And the prospects? That promotion you were hoping to get?" And when he didn't reply: "They want you to go and they make you a generous offer. If you don't accept it, you're not going to be very popular, are you?" She brought it to the point. "What are you going to do, Tom?"

"Oh, I think in the long run I shall decide to accept it," he answered largely.

"And?"

"Well, I don't know." He reached for his pipe and the pouch in Exiles colours. This was another thing she had come to realise – that he wasn't, as Sam had been, a compulsive smoker; that smoking as often as not was done to cover up an awkward moment.

"I might go into business," he said at length.

"What sort of business, Tom?"

"Well, I don't know. I need to give it a lot of thought. There's no real hurry."

She saw time stretching ahead, the weeks drifting by as the last few months of grace expired, the weeks racing by after they had expired, the thousand pounds gratuity and the little she had left in the Post Office slowly but steadily being eaten into. Tom in flannels and blazer at the Brownswood chatting,

Pickwickian-like, to his admirers about the marvellous opportunities this lucky break had opened up and the plans which he was formulating.

And she saw farther still, beyond the time when any enterprises in which he risked the thousand pounds had failed – for she knew instinctively that fail they would. They would be left with two pounds a week and Tom would have to find another job. At a time when unemployment, after falling a little from last year's woeful figures, had suddenly started to rise alarmingly, and, according to the pundits of gloom, was heading for the roof. What sort of job *could* he find? A man who had been trained to send coded messages to Hong Kong and Singapore and very little else. What had he to offer in competition with the millions who would be clamouring for the occasional posts available? She searched her mind and came up with very little. He was well read – he could talk books all day long when he had someone to talk them to, though he hadn't had anyone since he'd broken with Sam. Books. Public libraries? She shook her head. There'd be waiting lists for jobs with them already. Then how about with the new twopenny libraries? A lot of them were opening; they were getting popular. Yes, but not for the sort of books that Tom had talked to Sam about; it wasn't Johnson, Thackeray and Emerson, nor even Oscar Wilde the public were clamouring to read. It was the newer ones, which he disdained: Michael Arlen, Agatha Christie, Dorothy Sayers.

Then sport? Something to do with games? He was brilliant at anything that concerned a ball. It could be oval, round, small or large – it didn't matter. It was said at Belmont he'd made a hundred break at billiards using a broomstick! That if he took up golf he'd be playing to scratch within a season. Could he be a golf professional? Or a tennis coach? Or a sports master?

Sports master!

Yes! Why not? She sat bolt upright in the settee of which they were occupying corners.

"Tom," she said. "Couldn't you get a job as a sports master at one of the public schools? I mean you've had the right background, the right education. You could teach them . . . well, I don't know. English, I suppose. Or French. You say you're good at French—"

"Micky," he overrode her, "you just don't know what you're talking about. You have to be *fluent* in a language, not just good at it. Anyway, would you want to be a schoolmaster's wife?"

"I was talking about a sports master."

"Same thing. Only worse." He chuckled. "Poor old Captain Grimes."

"You mean Captain Elliott, don't you?"

He shook his head of thick, wavy, golden hair, his blue eyes glinting with determined confidence. "Grimes," he said. "Evelyn Waugh. *Decline and Fall.*"

"Tom, I don't know what you're talking about."

"New book that came out last year. Very clever. It's a satire on small private schools that are run on profit principles rather than tradition."

"Like St Olive's?"

It stopped him in his tracks. The easy manner vanished like blown mist. His eyes were of a sudden smaller and held the hint of cruelty she'd seen before.

"Now, listen, Micky—"

But she would not be overborne. "No, Tom," she said. "Let me have my say. It isn't much of a school, St Olive's, is it? I mean, it isn't really a preparatory school. Not one to prepare children for public schools. It's no more and no less than what you've just said: a school run for profit. I didn't realise that when we sent Dessy and Thady there, but from reading their letters, listening to what they tell us . . ." She paused, then took a gigantic risk.

"Tom," she said. "You didn't go to a proper preparatory school, did you?" And when he looked hard at her, barely able to hold her gaze, and didn't answer: "If you had, you'd have seen through St Olive's at first glance. In fact I doubt if you'd even have gone to look it over." And, deciding she might as well be hung for a sheep as for a lamb, "And you didn't go to a public school either, did you? Not the kind Sam went to, for example? Or Mott?"

His eyes blazed with a sudden, curious, helpless anger. "Don't you compare me with that bloody Jew!" he shouted.

She held her ground. "I'm not."

He got to his feet. "I don't intend to sit here and be insulted!" With the room serving as both sitting room and dining room, the dining table was very near. Taking a pace, he slammed a massive fist on its solid surface, making the laid cutlery shiver. "And," he went on, still shouting, his eyes very small, now shaking a fist at her, "I don't intend to be told how to run my affairs by a woman. It might have been all right for Sam Jordan but it isn't all right for me!"

He crossed to the door, opened it and stood for a moment looking at her. She saw the misery in his eyes and was ashamed at what she'd done but had been forced to do.

"What are you going to do, Tom?" she asked – but could have given the answer for him.

"I'm going for a drink! And don't expect me back before closing time!"

2

When he had gone, slamming the door behind him, Alice waited, listening to his footsteps down the stairs, anticipating and hearing the slam of the second door on the half landing which gave the flat its privacy. Then she went into the kitchen and turned the potatoes off. Because she didn't drink – except perhaps for a sip of wine on special occasions – she put the kettle on for a cup of tea, made it, and took it back into the sitting room.

There were, she appreciated, differences, but in essentials she was exactly back to that day nearly eight years before, in that ghastly room in number five Stradbroke Road, that hideous room with the Slit in which she'd had to house her babies, driven to distraction by a husband's refusal to face up to their situation. The room in which she had smashed the only worthwhile possession left to her and Sam out of their former affluence – the clock from Crogellan House given to them as a wedding present by Sam's mother, the gilt and marble clock which by its very inappositeness in such a sordid bed-sitting-room had shrieked the death of all her hopes and dreams.

She had recovered from that situation, slowly, painfully, wearily, entirely by her own efforts. Sam had encouraged, comforted, endured ill humours, unreasonableness, complaints. But not one finger had he raised to help in the essential restructuring of their lives. He had made his contribution: the four pounds a week which Mott paid him as a typewriter salesman and that had been, so far as he was concerned, the end of it. His conscience clear, he could go back to his bridge! And she had succeeded. By lying, forging references, cheating, plagiarising, beguiling and by sheer hard work she had risen through window dresser to dress designer and from dress designer to gown manufacturer. She had paid off the debts, got out of Stradbroke Road into decent rooms in Belmont proper. Had done well enough to be admired and envied by the Belmont set, to afford to dress herself and her children decently, take holidays, share in the madcap excitement all around her, see any revue or play she wanted to, try any restaurant. She had never looked back. There had been nothing to prevent her continually expanding until she became one of the country's household names. Everyone had told her that: Culverwell, Sam, Hetty – even Joseph Mott. And she had abandoned it. Thrown it away in exchange for a 'normal' way of life and a home in which to bring up her children.

And here she was, eight years on, back where she had started with another husband who would not face realities. One who, rather than do so, picked a quarrel and stormed out to some stinking pub; a husband who would henceforth contribute not four, but two pounds a week and play rugger or tennis instead of bridge! She had her two children but to be honest, she was as much apart from them as she had been in any of those eight long years. True, she had a home of sorts, part furnished, the attic rooms still much as they had been when they moved in because, after all, why bother when most of the time Dessy and Thady were away at boarding school and one hundred and three was just a stop gap anyway? But against a home she had to offset what she had lost. She had been an individual, a woman of consequence in an ideal situation to share to any extent she pleased the excitement of an age which promised new excitements every day; she had known a freedom such as she had never known before, the freedom to do exactly as she liked, to make decisions, good or bad, exactly as she chose; and she had had security at a time when security was a rare and precious thing. And she had cast these things aside as if they had been the merest trifles in exchange for a man who, with every day that passed, was proving himself a lesser man than the one she had given up for him, in exchange for a home and a way of life which, if something drastic wasn't done, would crumble away to dust.

The country was suddenly in a mess again – there was no escaping *that* reality. The papers were full of it, the wireless was full of it. They even talked about it at the Brownswood. But the country being in a mess was only vaguely disquieting when your husband was in full employment with every hope of advancement – it was only when that bastion of security was shattered that you were brought up short and really felt you had to *think* about it.

But she knew so little. When she had been in Belmont, living with a man with an enquiring mind and, more importantly, an open mind, who not only read the papers but analysed what was printed in them, argued the views expressed, put forward his own suggestions, often as no more than Aunt Sallys to be knocked about by all and sundry, she had been reasonably informed. But now she knew better the arguments as to the side the MCC should pick against these West Indian cricketers – who in spite of fierce objections from some quarters were apparently coming over this spring – than those about what should be done about the country's economy.

Lloyd George! He'd got an idea. What was it? Building lots of roads! Well, what good would that be to them? Tom could hardly take up navvying! Anyway, Lloyd George wasn't in power now and this new man, Churchill, who was Chancellor of the Exchequer, didn't think much of the idea and Stanley Baldwin said that if you left it alone, unemployment would go away of its own accord in the next five years. By which time Dessy would be sixteen and Thady fourteen. Public school? If something wasn't done they'd be lucky to be schooled at all. Lucky to see their time out at St Olive's even. Poor little mites! The words were by now so firmly lodged in her head, she couldn't get rid of them. She'd had such plans for them. And so, to be fair, had Tom. And it wasn't his fault he was going to lose his job.

Restlessly, her tea undrunk, forgotten, she paced the room and then under some compulsion went up to the attic floor. Going into their bedroom she switched on the light, which cast her shadow across the empty, made-up double bed and threw the room's bleak harshness into crude reality. She was ashamed. Her father had only been a railwayman and after his injury a ticket collector but she'd at least had lino on her bedroom floor. And there'd been five of them, not two! It was all very well making the excuse that one-o-three was just a stopgap but she should have been able to give them something better. Be honest, she told herself, it's been too many theatres, too much tennis and dancing, too many picnics and days of punting on the river and the children out of mind, safely tucked away in Wormley.

3

It was eleven o'clock before Tom came back. He was very drunk and for the first time Alice was fully to realise the awful metamorphosis liquor allied with self-doubt wrought in Tom Fenwick, turning him from a good-humoured, likeable and reasonable man into a surly, trouble-seeking bully. This change, she was to discover in the months which lay ahead, was not always immediate – there could be an intervening phase, as now, when he arrived, as it were, bearing gifts and was invested with a false breeziness, a cigarette drooping from the corner of his mouth, a lick of damp hair fallen across his forehead, his full cheeks dimpled with a determined grin.

"Brought you something, Micky," he announced with pride, holding out a small bottle which Alice took to be a miniature liqueur.

"Well, you can take it back where you got it from!" she snapped.

"Feller will have gone."

"You're drunk!" Alice dismissed him with contempt.

"Not drunk. Tight perhaps. Here." He shook the bottle at her as if he was ringing a small bell. "Good stuff. 'Spensive."

She snatched the bottle from him. On the flattened inset circle of its face was a label with a maker's name she had never heard of and the legend 'Attar of Roses'.

"Perfume," he explained.

She threw the bottle fiercely to the floor. Surprisingly it didn't break but bounced back towards her foot. She kicked it angrily away and it rattled against the skirting.

"Now you listen to me, Tom Fenwick!" she assailed him. "If

you think I'm going to put up with you going out and getting drunk every time—"

"Not drunk. Tight . . ."

"Every time you've got a problem facing you—"

"Problem?" He was affronted. "Haven't got a problem in the world."

"You haven't got a problem! What about losing your job? Don't you call that a problem?"

"Wass a job? Jobs for mugs. This feller . . . feller who gave me that" – his eyes, made smaller by the alcohol he'd absorbed, searched vaguely for the sample bottle of scent – "he's setting up on his own. Jus' wants a bit of capital to make a go of it."

"A bit of capital!" She clenched her fists so hard the nails dug into her palms. Her arms were rigid by her sides, her eyes fixed on his with mingled horror and disbelief. "Are you telling me, Tom Fenwick," she fumed, "that you've told someone you've just met in a pub that you're going to put some of the money you're going to get out of the Eastern Telegraph Company into some business to do with . . . with muck like that!?"

"'S not muck," he complained. "Good stuff. Here . . ." Off balance, he took a pace towards the bottle he had now espied and, but for the wall saving him, would have fallen.

"You're digusting!" Alice raged, stamping her feet. "A drink-sodden mess. As for going into business—"

"Got to." He had straightened himself but was still lolling against the wall. "There's the kids. Good kids. Bit soft . . ." He saw the glint in her eyes. "Under . . . standable." And, liking the word: "Very under . . . standable. But good stuff there. Need knocking into shape, thass all. When they get to their public school . . ."

"Public school!" Her voice rang out with prodigious derision. "Who do you think you're talking to? Your cronies in the Highbury Barn? That bunch of . . . of sychophants at the Brownswood Tennis Club? Your boozy chums in the Exiles

Rugger Club? *How* are they going to go to public school? Who's going to pay for it? Anyway, what do *you* know about public schools? You've never been to one. You're just a . . . a . . . a casuist. That's what you are, Tom Fenwick, a casuist!"

"A cas . . . cas . . ." He gave up the struggle. "It's a man who—"

"I know what it means! And if I don't, you know what I mean. Or would if you weren't too drunk! Well, it's no good talking to you. I'll talk to you in the morning when you're sober. And don't think you're coming into my bedroom, because you're not. As for this . . ."

She bent to pick up the sample with the intention of throwing it at him but was arrested by a sudden hand grabbing her arm in a vice-like grip. She turned her head. His face was not a foot from hers and of a sudden she was looking at a man she hadn't known existed, a man whose mood had, in an instant, utterly changed. A man indignant that his well-meaning attempt to bury the hatchet, shake hands, make up, had been spurned; a man wounded in pride; a man shown up a charlatan; a man despised, dismissed, degraded; above all a man trapped in a situation from which he knew only the one route of escape. Startled, Alice, staring into eyes turned pig-like, read, magnified, the same cruel streak she had occasionally glimpsed before and obstinately put from her mind. Through the thin stuff of her dressing gown she felt his enormous strength. He could, she knew, have strangled her without the slightest difficulty. But she was not afraid. Fear is an affection related to experience and so far as men were concerned, Sam Jordan, in that first dramatic rescue of her in a Warrington alleyway, had chased fear of men away – and in all the years which had elapsed since then, no man had frightened her.

So her eyes blazed with hurt and anger, not with fear.

"Let go of me!" she cried. "Let go my arm!"

A curious expression crossed his face, a mixture of wrath and bafflement. "I don't have a woman tell me where to sleep!" he shouted. And, absurdly: "I pay the rent!"

But he released her and she stood, somehow fragile-looking, in her nightdress and dressing gown, slowly rubbing her arm where he had gripped it.

"What I have I hold!" he yelled, even more loudly than before. "Do you understand, woman? Once and for all, do you understand!? What I have I hold!"

"I don't," she replied with sovereign contempt, "know what you're talking about."

"You're not married to Sam Jordan now!" His choler seemed at least to be giving him control over his speech. His face was scarlet, his forehead bedewed with sweat, his hands were shaking. "You hear me! *Ecce homo!* Behold, the man!" He bent his right arm and, holding his clenched fist before her face, gripped his bicep with the other hand. "Don't you try running me! Not Tom Fenwick!"

She read him correctly. The one advantage he had over her was his enormous strength. But he could not use it because he dared not use it. He lacked the mental courage to do what his emotions urged: to exert his mastery by sending her, with one blow of his arm, crashing to the floor. Yes, I was right, she told herself with a strange faint glow of triumph. Tom Fenwick is a coward. She believed his claim to have rescued Tappenden from drowning. She accepted that you could ask him to open an innings against England's fastest bowler and he would do so eagerly. In a rugger ruck he would take a battering with the best of them. A burglar breaking in would do so at his peril. But he was incapable of dealing with situations which required the exercise of moral courage. That was the fundamental weakness in his nature. That was why he drank. If she stayed with him she must be aware of this and all that flowed from it. He must face the years ahead knowing he lacked the mental stamina to deal with crises; that he would be useless whenever there were important decisions to be made; that she was, in these respects, as much on her own as she had ever been.

"You look stupid," she told him, facing the clenched fist unafraid. "And you talk stupidly. I'll speak to you in the morning when you're sober."

"Don' think you can keep me out of my bedroom," he shouted slurringly, making a pace after her as she turned to go. "I'll sh . . . shmash the door down if you try."

"And you would." She said it with terrible disgust. "But you don't have to because I'm going to sleep in Dessy's room."

She did not sleep at all that night but she did not, as she had on the wakeful periods of the previous occasion, spend it analysing herself and the man she had married. There was just one thing she had to think about – one simple question to answer, did she or did she not break with Tom?

She was not thinking of divorce. A second divorce so soon after the first was unthinkable, even if possible. To achieve it, Tom would have to be persuaded to agree to spending a night with some woman. She couldn't go through all that again; the meetings with solicitors and counsel, the drawing of petitions, the employment of a detective to keep watch on some sordid little hotel where Tom would be spending the night ostensibly committing adultery with a prostitute, the hiring of false witnesses, the subpoenas, letters, phone calls. The whispers, sidelong looks, the sudden silences. The tawdriness. The uncertainty and delay. The fresh crop of half truths or downright lies she'd have to devise to satisfy Dessy and Thady's puzzlement and curiosity; the bewilderment of Ma and Pa; the searching enquiries by Hetty. And then at the end, as likely as not, some judge refusing to divorce them!

No, divorce was out – or at least out for quite some time to come.

But she *could* leave him. Move back into Cranmore temporarily and accept Culverwell's offer to go back to working for him as a dress designer. Or even borrow another two hundred and fifty pounds from him and start a new Paquette. If he'd lend it. It wasn't certain that he would – not when by refusing he would be putting pressure on her to work for him instead of for herself. And even if he did lend her the money, oh, the effort it would require! The first time had been one thing – she'd been full of the thrill of a brand new enterprise, ignorant of what was involved. But now she could see it all, clearly and depressingly. The slow grind of building up again from nothing. The worry of fending off creditors while trying to skewer money out of clients without offending them, perhaps even losing them, by over-prompt demands for payment. She had no doubt of her ability to succeed, even in these straitened times, but oh, for the cushion of sufficient cash to see her through that first difficult twelve months or so.

And Tom would before very long be getting that thousand pounds. Left to his own devices he'd fritter it away or have it filched off him by some confidence trickster in the Grenadier or the Highbury Barn. But if she could lay her hands on it! With what she had herself it would be more than enough to start her new Paquette!

Her imagination kindled, her psyche inflamed, she could not longer lie in bed. Risking splinters she paced the narrow confines of the attic bedroom, walking back and forth, bending her head at each extremity to avoid bumping against the sloping ceiling before finally taking up her stance at the tiny window which, from four and a half floors up, looked down on the sleeping emptiness of Highbury New Park. She waited impatiently for dawn, her mind half occupied with future plans and half wondering, guiltily, about her children banished to St Olive's.

Six

1

"Be quiet."

Awakened out of a heavy sleep, Thady Jordan stared, puzzled, at the shape between him and the dormitory window. He could not at first translate it as that of a human being. It was simply a mass which cut off the faint night glow. He began to mutter something but a hand placed across his mouth choked off his speech.

"I said, be quiet!" The hissed whisper held a frightening menace.

He felt the hand removed.

"There's nothing to be frightened of," he heard. "Just do what I tell you."

He knew who it was: Morris Sams. To each of the dormitories, Mrs Latham had allocated to be responsible for keeping order one of the several far older boys who, remarkably, were still being educated at St Olive's.

It did not occur to Thady to do anything but obey.

He felt the cool of the night air as the coverlets were drawn back off him and heard the creaking of the bed springs as Morris Sams climbed in beside him.

"Lie on your front and pull your pyjamas down."

The command was whispered directly into his ear from two or three inches' distance. Uncomprehendingly he did as he was ordered and the next thing he knew was that

Sams had lifted himself up and was lying on top of him and something huge was being thrust inside him.

"Keep quiet. It'll hurt a bit, first time, but keep absolutely quiet."

Bewildered, terrified, Thady dared not make a sound.

The pain was awful, searing, as the thing was pushed further and further into him and then began to move slowly up and down varying the degree of pain. He could hear Sams' heavy breathing and the creaking of the bed which matched the slow and deliberate thrusts. He felt enveloped by a body far larger than his own which seemed to cut off everything, limiting the world to what was happening: to a heavy breathing, and a creaking, to the coming and going weight of a body against his own, to arms on either side of him grasping the bedhead, and to the mysterious agony. And as well he was aware of the extraordinary intimacy of the business with which nothing in his life before was to be compared. Even above the shock and pain of it, this, accompanied by a contrary sense of being overwhelmed, was as compelling as never afterwards to be forgotten; he was a thing which was being used and yet, paradoxically, a partner in a mysterious and inexplicable rite.

Later, when the shock of his being so brutally raped had dulled and he could mentally stand away from the happening and consider it, he instinctively knew it to be erotic without knowing what eroticism was. For years he had shared a bed with his brother and they had often slept locked in each others' arms, but the fusion in this terrible violation of his innocence was closer a thousand times than that had ever been. He knew, as almost without exception all small children know, the strange and delicious pleasure of masturbation and although not at the time sexually aroused by being buggered, when later, as time after time he reviewed this terrible experience, he knew intuitively that what had happened was of a cousinage. In that first swift rape of his virginity, sweet, unblemished childhood was left behind.

When Sams, with a final whisper that he must tell no one what had happened, had left him and gone back to his own bed in the corner by the window, sore, mystified, still not fully comprehending, Thady Jordan lay awake for a little while remembering something of what Sams had said to him – that it would hurt a bit first time – and realised that this thing was to be done to him again, perhaps often done to him again. Not for an instant did it occur to him that he could object; it never crossed his mind that he could complain or seek protection. Morris Sams was a big boy and this, presumably, was what big boys did to little boys whenever they felt like doing it. And indeed the events of succeeding weeks merely confirmed this assumption for Sams was catholic in his tastes and there were five little boys in the dormitory for him to choose amongst. Thady Jordan, like his contemporaries, could hear the creak of Sams as he quit his bed and wonder if it would be his turn tonight or Watson's, or Pountney's, Michelson's or Smith's. And if he was not chosen he would listen to the sounds of it going on, relieved to be spared the pain, yet curiously jealous that someone else had been preferred and conscious of the loneliness of his empty bed.

In fact only once more did Sams select Jordan as his instrument which was probably due to the good fortune of the position of his bed which was against the wall which separated Mrs Latham's bedroom from the dormitory. The wall was thin and Mrs Latham, apparently sleeping lightly, must have heard the creaking of the bed springs and called out demanding what was the noise in there? Sams froze, huge and heavy, and whispered to Thady to call out nothing was happening – which he did – and after a while Sams pulled himself out and went back to his bed and never tried to bugger him again. And in fact, for several nights, there was quiet in the dormitory.

Then, close to the end of term, the business came to an end for all the little boys when, during a lesson, one of the pupils who slept in another dormitory asked one of the masters how babies were born and Pountney, in an excess of enthusiasm to show his superior knowledge, volunteered: "Please, sir, I know. Morris Sams did it to me in bed last night." This elicited quite a buzz which the master swiftly checked and later that day Sams was observed leaving Mrs Latham's study red-eyed and angry. There was talk that he'd probably be expelled but he wasn't; after all, the fees his parents were paying were as good as anyone else's. He was shifted to another far bigger dormitory and whether or not he sodomised any of the little boys in that one too, Thady Jordan never knew.

2

The afternoon following the Pountney incident there was an end-of-term cricket match on Great Field in which Desmond was playing. Thady sat on the grass watching, hoping that when the side his brother was playing on was batting he would find a way of speaking to him. As is usually the case with brothers at the same school who are significantly separated in age, they had little contact; it was, Desmond had once patiently, if somewhat loftily, explained, rather *infra dig* for seniors and juniors to be pally. In fact this was something of a cover-up for there was in Desmond's case a more justifiable reason – his size. He had a beautifully proportioned body but it was small in scale and for all his extra two years he was still slightly smaller than his brother so that, as he saw it, to be bracketed with Thady would be to run the risk of being regarded by his peers as a junior as well. However, the fact of being one of the only twenty-two wearing white flannels conferred a distinction and permitted an exception to be made without undue loss of face and besides, there were questions he wanted answered. He sank down in the long grass beside Thady willingly enough.

"Do *you* know how babies are made, Desmond?" Thady asked.

This was difficult. In a vague sort of way, Desmond thought he knew. It was something to do with girls. But basically Desmond knew very little about girls and nothing at all about their anatomy. Since their departure from kindergarten school, the Jordan boys had scarcely met one. They had been the only children in Belmont Hotel – the solitary exception that Mrs Latta, seduced by their father's charm, had allowed. And it had never occurred to a father utterly absorbed in contract bridge or a mother with her energies split between business and sharing in the frenzy of the twenties to do anything about repairing this omission. It was true there had been girls in Liverpool but at school they had separate playgrounds and out of school hopscotch and stilt-walking were masculine prerogatives. By the time he found himself at a school where other boys had at least a smattering of knowledge on the subject, Desmond, quickly realising his ignorance and having to bear in mind his smallness and the curious fact of his having a different surname from his parents, wisely decided it was safer to perpetuate his greenness rather than admit to it – to repeat the slang was easier than to enquire into its meaning.

"You do it with your prick," he said. "You must know that."

"That's what Pountney said." What Pountney had said had gone round the school like wildfire.

"Well, there you are."

"Could Pountney have a baby?"

"Don't be silly, Thady. Only ladies have babies."

"Why's that, Desmond?"

"Because it's the way they're made." And, hastily: "Inside."

"You mean if Pountney was made inside the way that ladies are made inside he could have a baby too because of what Morris Sams did to him?"

These were slippery grounds. And meanwhile the question Desmond wanted the answer to was burning in his mind. "He's not old enough," he temporised. "You have to be grown up to have a baby."

"Aunt Hetty's grown up and she hasn't had any babies," Thady pointed out.

"Don't be silly. You have to be married to have babies."

Thady pulled out a long piece of grass and chewed it thoughtfully. That was quite right. Aunt Hetty wasn't married and hadn't had any babies. Not at least so far as he knew. And she had never talked to him about them if she had.

"Do they give ladies something when they get married, then, so that they can have a baby?" he asked, puzzled.

"It's nothing like that, silly," Desmond said, somewhat contradicting his earlier statement. "Ladies can have babies without being married but it's very bad if they do and they get sent to prison."

"Oh." Thady stared through the high grass and across the cricket pitch to the Victorian enormity of the school partially screened by tall trees, feeling a stab of dismay.

"If Pountney had a baby because of what Morris Sams did to him, would they send him to prison?" he asked timidly.

"I told you, Thady, only ladies can have babies."

"Yes, but if . . . if it . . ." He didn't know how to put it. "If it went wrong and Pountney did have a baby somehow, would they send him to prison?"

Desmond was exasperated. "It's like asking what would happen if one of those trees started to walk towards us." He pointed to the line of poplars between the edge of the playing field and the river. "It's a silly question." And to escape from the morass he came out with his question baldly. "Did Morris Sams do it to you as well?"

Thady nodded. "He did it to all of us."

"What was it like?"

"It hurt. Almost as much as being caned. Only different."

"Why didn't you tell him to stop doing it then?"

"No one did. Well, I never heard them."

"You could have told Doctor Donleavy. Or Captain Elliott. Or Mrs Latham."

"That would have been sneaking."

Desmond nodded thoughtfully. "Yes."

"Anyway Morris Sams said he'd do dreadful things to us if we did."

"What things?"

"He didn't say. But terrible things."

"He didn't do anything to Pountney."

"No," Thady agreed. "Do you have anybody in your dorm who does it?"

Desmond shook his head. Small though he was, his demeanour was in keeping with his neatness, his bearing excellent, his gestures economical. They were still astonishingly alike, their blue eyes set well apart and framed by curling eyelashes, their faces chubby and well-complexioned, their chins, like their father's, already positive. Desmond was entitled to be concerned at being seen hobnobbing with his brother: to newcomers they looked like twins.

"I don't think so," he said. "Greene says it's a very naughty thing to do." Greene was a Morris Sams equivalent. "Well," he went on, making a slight correction, "Greene says it's a naughty thing to do to other boys but it's all right doing it to girls when you get older."

This was totally beyond Thady's imagination. He was proud of and very interested in his penis, a useful appurtenance which he was inclined to regard as something living and distinct from the rest of him. It could be useful for firing pennies a very considerable distance – only the other day he had managed to clear the wall between the disused greenhouses and the out-of-bounds bit of ground, which was more than Michelson had been able to do; it was the only part of him which could change size; and it could give you feelings which were exciting and quite unlike anything else in the world. He often masturbated even thought he knew – although how he knew he couldn't have said – that it was a bad thing to do and some of the boys said that you could give yourself terrible diseases or even go blind by doing it which was frightening. But he did it without conjuring up concomitant images of girls although he knew from what the other boys whispered that it and girls were supposed to be connected. And now here was Greene, who was big enough to be regarded as something of a demi-god, saying you could do this with it as well and it was all right to do it when you were older. It was very interesting and for some reason made his heart beat a little faster.

"How old have you got to be, Desmond?" he asked eagerly. "Did he tell you?" His brother shook his head. "Is *he* old enough to do it?" And, before there could have been a response. "Do you think Morris Sams does it to girls in the holidays? Or to his sister? He's got a sister, hasn't he? I wish we had a sister."

The click of wicket falling and a scattering of applause ended the discussion.

"Wyngarde's out," Desmond said, getting to his feet. "I'm in next but one."

Thady was left with too many things to think about to be interested in the cricket. He watched Desmond make his way towards a small knot of other white-flannelled older boys and then, lying on his stomach, wriggled his way through the long grass towards the river. Great Field was bounded by horizontal iron railings and on the other side of them the ground sloped down towards the New River. It was out of bounds and if you were caught there it meant a whacking, but with the match in progress the chances of getting away with it were good. The lowest rail was high enough above the ground to squeeze through below and he made the level pathway which ran alongside the stream unobserved although rather badly stung by nettles lurking in the grass.

The only river he had ever got close to before coming to St Olive's had been the Mersey which was tidal and muddy, whereas the New River was crystal clear and very tranquil. Artificially created, unusable by traffic, unsullied by effluents, it flowed evenly, its surface hardly a nose length below its trim, grassy banks. After the hard Highbury pavements and the cobbled alleyways of Liverpool where most of his waking hours away from adults had been spent, it seemed to him to be far more than a river, to be a mythic flow within which one could lose oneself and discover a brand new world in which there were no problems. He would lie, small enough to fit on the narrow margin beside the stream, his head so close to its surface as to sense the shift of it, watching the darting minnows and the water-beetles, imagining he was there with them below the surface, living with them amongst the trailing weeds, knowing a life without lessons and canings and being in trouble if you didn't eat things you hated. He never spoke of this communion to the other boys, not even to his brother. To be here was a secret joy and an escape from unhappiness and confusion.

But today he didn't lie belly down on the margin and gaze into the river but did something he hadn't dared risk doing before, which was to walk along until he came to the footbridge which led to the wood growing all along the opposite bank. Not only was the wood out of bounds but it was private property and there was a notice which said that trespassers would be prosecuted. He had never been tempted to explore it before but now he hardly hesitated. He had never been in a wood before and although his mind was astir with all manner of worrying thoughts, the wonder of it wasn't lost on him. Kicking his feet gloriously through fallen leaves and debris, snagged now and then by brambles and by creepers, he plunged deep in until he came to a sort of clearing where a fallen tree offered a place to sit and ponder on what Desmond had just told him. Even so for quite some little time he sat looking about him, listening to the rustling of the leaves, looking at the patterns of dappled sunshine, smelling the scent of rotting wood and fresh green growth and honeysuckle, and, in spite of vague qualms about snakes or dangerous animals which might suddenly materialise to gobble him up, was rapt in the magic of it all.

But there were matters to be considered and time was limited. Reluctantly he closed his mind to the things around him and, undoing his shorts, pulled out his penis and examined it. Perhaps more than ever before he saw it not as part of himself but as something which had a separate existence. Dimly he realised that it was something which had a social value, that it was to do with manhood. All boys had pennies, or pricks as they were sometimes called, but they couldn't make babies with them. Only grown-ups could do that. And then only with girls. Not with boys. Which was jolly lucky because otherwise Morris Sams might have made a baby inside himself. It was an awe-inspiring and totally baffling thought. If Morris Sams *had* been able to make a baby in him, how would it get out? But of course it didn't apply. Only ladies had babies. Well, how did they get out of ladies? Maybe it was something to do with belly buttons which little girls had as well as boys and were something else no one had explained. He pulled up his shirt and began to examine his belly button as carefully as he had his penis . . .

A small boy of eight, seated on a fallen tree trunk, grappling with the mysteries of sexuality almost as a blind man might grapple with the mystery of colour.

Except in this: that Sams, in selecting Thady Jordan as a victim for his sodomy, had forced him to live, even if uncomprehendingly, his first truly erotic experience and had, by doing so, if in the most unhappy way, opened the door on a stream of consciousness of which, until then, he had been entirely ignorant.

Seven

1

For Alice the passing months were as difficult and frustrating as any she had known. Tom, having once conceived the notion of using his severance compensation to set himself up in some sort of business, was not easy to dissuade. He was, she realised, in desperate need of the reassurance which he found amongst those who claimed his friendship in the Highbury Barn; with these men of lesser intelligence, lesser education and lesser means, he could more than hold his own. It would be balm to his hurt pride to hear their calls of welcome ring out as he came in through the saloon bar door; reassuring to be able to lean nonchalantly on the counter declaring his views with little fear of disagreement; satisfying to talk largely, if not specifically, of his commercial plans. These were worrying and perplexing days of growing unemployment with the shadow of bankruptcy hanging over the land; a man who was not only prepared to buy drinks all round but was clearly going to be able to do so for quite some time to come was a rare and welcome companion.

Alice came to know the suspense of women who await such a man's return, wondering if it would be the clear-headed husband packed off for work that morning or some fuddled drunk. She soon learnt to judge his state exactly from his approaching footsteps up the stairs and know that when they were slow and determined the opening door would disclose a creature utterly transformed, a swaying sot, a cigarette drooping wetly from his lips, ash patterning his jacket, his wavy hair flattened by sweat, his eyes at once defensive and belligerent. As like as not there would be in his hand some useless peace offering, a crushed bunch of flowers, a box of chocolates or, most frequently, yet another sample of cheap perfume. There seemed no limit to the varieties available: attar of roses, jasmine, violet, patachouli, musk. She got to loathe the stink of them all. They permeated the flat, even somehow the bread board, so that any slice cut on it from a loaf was redolent with scent.

Sometimes, driven beyond self-control by her criticism and contempt, he struck her, but little by little as the weeks passed by and her appraisal of his character became more accurate, her ability to judge how far she could go in slating him without risking physical hurt became astonishingly precise. While he had a swift and frightening temper, which was most easily aroused by mockery, there was a craven streak in him which held him back from giving total vent to it. A woman who could never accept passivity, Alice stood her ground; taunting him became her chosen method of revenge for the carefully cooked dinner cold and wasted, for the shame of knowing that Colonel and Mrs Warburton in the flat beneath could hear his bellowing, for the chagrin of discovering just what she had got for herself in exchange for Sam Jordan and Paquette.

And there was something else: in holding her own while he ranted and raged, threatened and blustered, she was affirming her independence. Had she not resisted, had she succumbed to tears and pleas, to the contemporary acceptance of male dominance in marriage, she knew her spirit would soon be crushed and nothing but inescapable disaster would lie ahead of her.

The alternatives remained: to leave him or manage him. She decided on the latter, partly because he was, when not in drink, a perfectly reasonable companion, and partly because of the covenanted golden handshake. If that thousand pounds was going to go into any business, it was going to be her business it was going into. The time to break with him, if there was to be a time, would be when she was re-established.

But he was obstinate and she understood why. Whatever the front he showed to other people, he knew himself. The absurd presents he returned with from his drinking bouts were, she knew, more than mere peace offerings; they were tacit admissions of guilt for his own weakness and vulnerability. She soon realised that he didn't drink because he was an alcoholic but simply to fend off uncertainty. He did not intend to become inebriated and found no pride in being so and, once out of the company of his drinking cronies, far from being exhilarated, was quarrelsome and morose. The abrupt termination of his career with the Eastern Telegraph Company, soon to become effective, had been a shattering blow and, utterly lost as to what he should do with his working life instead, he gratefully clung to the chimera of merchant adventurer. Just as alcohol saw him through an evening, so did grandiose imaginings see him through the dreadful months while he waited for the axe actually to fall.

Alice realised she must apply all her skills, that she must be patient and use his weaknesses to promote her ends. She must stand her ground without carrying this so far as to provoke a breach impossible to bridge; he must not leave for work next morning smouldering with rancour. A measure of flattery would dull the edge of the previous evening's scorn. And in any case she had, meanwhile, to get on with living. Common sense told her that there was simply no point in resuscitating yesterday's quarrel when today's man was rational and affectionate. On the contrary, since his desire for her was strong, morning was the time to signal that if he came home sober her body would be available.

2

Tom's final stint of night duty was to occur a couple of weeks before the boys were due home for the summer holidays after the completion of their first full year at St Olive's. Especially in the summer months, Alice had never really minded Tom's night duty which brought with it its own particular pattern of life, with him sleeping through the morning, leaving the afternoon free for tennis when the weather was suitable. Now, with instant dismissal being the penalty for any Eastern operator found affected by alcohol when on duty, these spells, usually of ten days' duration, stood out as pleasant islands in uneasy seas and Alice resolved to profit by the last of them.

With the bathroom next to the kitchen she was able to chat with him as he finished his midday ablutions.

"Tom," she said, busy with the frying pan, "why don't we go on the river? It's such a lovely day."

"What?" In his pyjama bottoms he stepped into the little hallway, chin lathered, shaving brush in hand.

"I wondered if for a change we might go on the river instead of playing tennis?"

He looked at her with delight. She had recently changed her hair-style. It was still bobbed but loosely waved and combed back from her forehead, giving her an even more feminine look. The dress which she had carefully chosen was new and stylish, and softer too, its loose neckline falling in graceful curves across her chest.

"Yes, Micky, why not?" he agreed eagerly. "We could go to Richmond or Maidenhead. Yes, why not Maidenhead? We could get a punt. Pole up through Boulter's Lock. Then come back and have tea at Skindles."

"Have we time?"

"Oh, plenty. The trains are very good. Stick a couple of sausages in the pan to keep the inner man from grousing."

"I'll do some fried potatoes too," she said. "Make a brunch of it."

"Are you happy, dear?"

Alice, recumbent on cushions, looked up at him against the background of Maidenhead Bridge and white fluffy clouds in a summer sky. Except that he was now rather overweight, Tom, in white flannels and open-necked white shirt with sleeves rolled up to the elbows, looked very much the part. He was an efficient punter and drove them along against the current with ease and grace; his massive forearms, glinting with golden hairs, spoke of his strength, his bearing showed the confidence he felt whenever he was doing something for which he had a natural talent.

"Yes, Tom," Alice said. "I'm very happy."

And it was true enough. If only, Alice mused, life could always go on like this, could be days of blue skies and hot sunshine and a man who cared for her and had no drink inside him – and there were no such things as grocer's bills and worries about the future.

"I'm a beast to you sometimes," Tom said. "I know that. But I love you, Micky."

"Yes, I know you do."

"I'm going to fight it down."

"Don't talk about it now, dear."

"No, I must. It's easier when I'm doing something." He thrust down hard, then allowed the pole to ride up easily in his hands. Alice trailed her fingers in the water on either side.

"I don't really drink all that much, you know. It's just that I haven't got the head for it."

This was a huge admission when the natural thing was for him to boast of his ability to hold his liquor.

"I only intend to have a pint of beer but you have to stand your round. And it sort of creeps up on you. And then you know you're getting tight and you're . . . well, it's easier staying than going home."

"Yes, I suppose it is."

"You're very good to me. I don't know why you haven't walked out on me months ago."

"It's only because you're worried, Tom. I realise that."

"Do you?" He paused long enough for the prow of the punt to swing round a trifle in the current. With a gentle sideways movement of the pole he corrected it – it was astonishing that a man so powerfully made could be so delicate. She noticed that not one drop of water twinkled on his knife-creased flannels. "I'm worried more for you, Micky, you know," he went on. "I promised you so much. And I meant those promises. It wasn't just hot air."

"I know."

"It's these damn bloodsuckers in the City. All they think about is making money. People don't matter to them. But I'm going to show them. You'll see. I'm going to make it up to you for the rotten things I've done. I'm going to give you everything there is to have. Like that." He was pointing to a car speeding past them on the road which ran beside the river. "We'll have one of those one day. And a house of our own. In the country. You'd like that, wouldn't you? To live in the country?"

Alice watched the car disappearing from view. She thought of the DKW she and Sam had once owned, of rolling along Nether Street in it dressed up to the nines like royalty. To own a car in those days had been to cut a very rare and special figure. Now? Well, it was still rather special but no longer remarkable.

She thrust the thought away. "I don't know, Tom," she said. "I've never lived in the country. I don't know if I'd like it really."

"You'd soon get used to it. And we wouldn't have to be *buried*. We could get a place somewhere near a market town. Guildford, perhaps. Or Crawley. It's a nice town, Crawley."

They were nearing Boulter's Lock and the gates were opening to let out a steam launch, a splendid thing of polished woodwork and glittering brass and a canted-back smoke stack. A gramophone aboard was playing 'Mean to Me'. Inside the glass-walled cabin, the captain in a rakish naval cap drove it dashingly one-handed, his other arm around the waist of his companion. In the stern a youth in a pale blue blazer was carefully coiling some brand-new rope while a girl with her cloche hat almost pulled down over heavily mascared eyes flashed long silken legs and languidly smoked a cigarette in a holder of quite ridiculous length

"What do I have to do?" asked Alice.

"You don't have to do anything," Tom answered masterfully. "You just lie there looking beautiful." He waved a hand as to an equal to the passing launch whose master showed faint surprise but nodded courteously.

"Can we have one of those as well?" said Alice, entering into the spirit of the thing.

"Of course. There's nothing in the world I'm not going to give you, Micky. Nothing in the whole wide world."

He poled into the lock, which, because it was a weekday, they had to themselves. He managed the business efficiently, laying the punt pole down, throwing the rope up to the lock keeper to put round the bollard and drop down to him, then, as the water was let in, pulling it taut all the time as they rose and allowing the prow to swing out a little against the flow. Alice enjoyed the buffet of the current against her hand and, liking the smell of the water, said so.

"Sweetly rotten, unforgettable, unforgotten," Tom said.

"What's that?"

"I think it's Rupert Brooke. Or maybe it was Tennyson."

Alice remembered that Tennyson had stayed at Crogellan

House with Sam's parents, but she said: "It would be nice to live on a river."

"They flood. There were terrible floods this year. Half Maidenhead was under water. And you get rheumatism when you get older. And most of the winter they're in fog." He wasn't looking at her, but at the front of the punt, keeping its prow meticulously correct. "Chap was telling me the other day – Eastern fellow – you can pick them up for a song, riverside properties."

Alice, who liked the turn of the conversation, said: "Where did you learn to punt so well, Tom?"

"Oh, it's a knack, you know. Sort of thing you can pick up or you can't."

Sam, Alice reflected, had been hopeless at it. They had tried it once and had gone round in circles and ended up by paddling.

"Like playing games, I suppose," she said. "Do you think there's a connection?"

"Well, I suppose balance comes into it . . ."

They went through the lock. For a little while the stream was canalised between the lock island and the road but soon it broadened, the road fell back and out of sight and there were open fields one side and the Cliveden woods the other.

"Why don't we pull in under the trees?" Tom suggested. "Out of the sun?"

"Already?"

"I'd like a pipe," he lied.

"Yes, dear," Alice agreed, unsuspectingly.

He moored it expertly, driving the pole deep into the river bed and tying the rope to an overhanging branch. It was pleasant here, the sun dappling through the trees, the wooded slopes rising steeply beside them, the stream flowing quietly past. Tom reached for his blazer and extracted pipe, pouch and matches. It was curious, Alice mused, how different a pipe looked on her two husbands. It had given Sam a sort of sparkle, the stem held easily between his teeth, the bowl projecting at an angle; with Tom it was . . . well, part of the equipment. It went with the Exiles blazer and the Old Reigatian tobacco pouch. And he didn't smoke it very much; it was always more in his hand than in his mouth. She suspected that he didn't really enjoy a pipe at all – or even cigarettes for that matter.

Lying back on the deep, soft cushions, watching the beech leaves fluttering above her, she was tempted to let her thoughts wander. She could have lain for hours like this, perfectly content, perhaps drifting off into a doze. But there were things to be decided; she mustn't lose this golden opportunity.

"Tom?"

"Yes, Micky?"

"Would *you* like it if we moved into the country?"

"Only if you would, dear."

"I expect Dessy and Thady would now that they must have got used to it at St Olive's. It would be nice, wouldn't it? We could keep chickens and things like that. And we could buy a house, couldn't we? Easily out of that thousand pounds you're going to get? There'd still be lots left over."

The remark caused Tom unease. It wasn't going to be a thousand pounds. There was still a small balance resulting from the Tappenden loan to be paid out of it and after paying off the astounding debts he'd kept running up at the Highbury Barn and elsewhere, there wouldn't be much more than five hundred.

"We'll have to hold our horses, Micky, for a bit. Until I've got things organised."

"We don't have too much time left, do we?"

"You're not to worry your pretty head. I've got a few irons in the fire. If it hadn't been for this damn Labour government, I'd have got it sorted out already."

Alice let it ride over her. The portents of the coming slump were only too clear. There was already a remark going the rounds that even men with degrees were going to be two a penny.

"I was thinking of the Hong Kong Shanghai Bank," Tom went on airily.

She couldn't believe her ears. "I'm not going to Hong Kong!" she expostulated. "Or Shanghai! What would we do about Dessy and Thady?"

"I'm not proposing to *live* out there," Tom said, chuckling. "No, they've got a branch in London. Well, it's the head office actually. They're on the lookout for likely staff."

"How do you know?"

"Tappenden's been looking into it."

Alice had met Percy Tappenden. Tall, dark, thin, his hair smarmed down in George Raft style, weak-looking, raddled. She had been anything but impressed. She had seen him as possibly Tom's evil genius as Joseph Mott had been Sam's. It had been one of her conditions in marrying Tom that he'd never bring the man into her home.

"You've been talking us over with Tappenden," she objected. "Oh, Tom! How could you?"

"Well, we're both in Electra House. I'm bound to see him now and then."

"I'm not talking about seeing him."

"Well, he's got some ideas. I mean apart from the HK and S. Good ideas."

A warning bell rang furiously. "To do with your compensation money? That's what you're talking about, isn't it?"

"He knows a lot of people, Micky." How on earth had he got himself into this mess? Why the hell had he dragged Tappenden into the conversation? He was always a red rag to a bull so far as Micky was concerned.

"What has he been suggesting to you?" She was sitting upright now.

"Well, he thinks there's a tremendous future in wirelesses."

"And what do you know about wirelesses?"

"Well, it's my business, Micky."

"It isn't your business at all. Your business is tapping out messages and decoding those that you receive."

"When we were at Porthcurno—"

"They trained you in wireless telegraphy."

"And we had to know how radio waves were sent out and received."

"And what has that to do with being in the wireless business?"

"Well," Tom said, with dignity. "Everything."

"And what exactly did Tappenden suggest you did in the wireless business? Made them? Or sold them?"

"It's something we're looking into . . ."

"You're looking into? You mean you and Tappenden?" She checked herself and, leaning forward, put a hand on his shin which was as far as she could reach. "Oh, Tom," she said. "I can understand you wanting to be your own boss. But it isn't that easy. I know. I've been in it." She paused, seeming to give it a lot of thought. "Tom." She was gazing deep into his eyes, finding them defensive and unsure, yet obstinate. Things were on a knife edge; they could go either way. "Tom," she said, "that's what you really want to do, isn't it? Be in business on your own account? Rather than in something where someone's telling you what you've got to do all the time?"

Tom nodded. This was better. "I wasn't made to toe the line at someone else's bidding. In the Eastern it's different. We're specialists. Every man jack of us. No one tells us what to do. But you're not going to catch me at some desk adding up a lot of figures at the beck and call of some jumped-up nobody!"

"It wouldn't be right for you," Alice agreed, reflecting that the life of the Hong Kong and Shanghai Bank had been a short one. "I know that." And, tellingly: "Quite apart from the fact that it's not going to be all that easy to get the right sort of post with things as they are these days. But if you're set on doing something of your own then I'd like to help you. I really would."

His eyes closed a trifle. "You're not seriously suggesting . . ." He disdained to finish it.

"Why not?" She shifted a little towards him. "Why not, Tom? It's the one thing between us we know something about."

He knocked out the dottle from his pipe into the passing stream. It made no fizz. It had been long since out.

"I did not marry you," he said sententiously, "to be kept by you as your previous husband was." He put down the pipe and moving towards her reached for her hand. "Micky, dear, I am not one of those men who think the husband has to rule the roost. I am the first to agree that marriage is a joint enterprise to which both husband and wife contribute. I promised you a home and I've given you one. Not much of a home, I agree. Not what I was hoping to give you and would have given you but for these Imperial and International Communications bloodsuckers! But still it is a home which is more than you had from Sam Jordan since that business he and Mott had went up the spout. And that's where a woman's place is, in the home. The husband's part in a marriage—"

"Yes, I know, dear," Alice interrupted hastily. "And it's not your fault at all things have worked out the way they have. And I'm not suggesting what you seem to think I am."

"Oh?" His wiry eyebrows came down in puzzlement.

"If you want to go into business, why *not* the dress business?"

"The rag trade! Me?"

Alice nodded. "Why not? I could help you get it started and then when you've . . . well, learnt the ropes, I could stop coming in. Or maybe just come in once or twice a week."

"But I don't know the first thing about it."

"Neither did I when I first started. And, Tom, if you knew

how when I had Paquette I longed to have someone help me make decisions. Someone who could stand between me and . . ." She paused. She had been about to say something unchristian about the people she had to do business with. "Between me and . . . oh, so many problems which a man could handle so much more easily than a woman. But Sam would have been quite useless. Anyway all he wanted to do was play bridge."

She had put her hand over his and was looking deep into his eyes. I wonder if I'm keeping what I'm really thinking out of mine, she asked herself. That the last thing I'd be able to bear would be to have him under my feet; that in the rag trade he'd be utterly useless; that the men and women of Little Titchfield Street would make rings round him. But she had enough belief in herself not to look away. In the Paquette years she'd learnt how to lie convincingly while conveying artlessness and how to beguile even the most hard-bitten of men. In comparison with them Tom was an *ingénue*.

And on her side?

Well, his objections were, she knew, neither well thought out nor even really deeply held. They were the simple prejudices of a man of stock notions; a man who clung almost religiously to the rules and maxims an unimaginative and unsympathetic father had inculcated and school had underlined. A woman's place was in the home. Man was the breadwinner. To be in trade was *infra dig*. A catalogue of bromides masquerading as convictions. Catchphrases convincing until challenged by circumstances or undermined by fear. Perhaps this last above all – because he was at heart fearful of the future and baffled as to the next step he should take.

And there was something else, something which maybe had not as yet properly sunk into his consciousness. That when in a few days' time he finished with the Eastern Telegraph Company he would not merely be unemployed, unearning, but be cut off from the one society in which he fitted.

"Tom," she said, "there's something else I know you must have thought about. Leaving the Eastern is in a way like leaving—" She had almost said 'school'. "Like leaving a career in the army. And maybe that's all right when you're old and ready to put your feet up. But in your case . . . You're going to miss all the friends you've made. The men you've seen every day for years and years. You're going to need something challenging to fill that gap . . ."

She had, unknowingly, chosen a propitious moment. The sight of the woman he loved so deeply lying back on the soft, deep cushions had stirred desire in him. On the whole he had retained an attitude towards sex which was very much in line with his attitudes to life: all South Americans were dagoes; made-up ties were only worn by cads; in making love exaggeration was to be avoided. The place to have sex with one's wife was in a bed and the proper way to do it was in the straightforward way. One was tempted to be perverted but yielding to such temptations was no more of an excuse than yielding to the triumph of winning a game by cheating. But to make love in a punt, with your wife . . . unusual, perhaps, but not abnormal. Permissable surely? And now, with Alice's hand in his, her eyes looking trustfully into his, the nearness of her, the intimacy of the setting, he set aside his doubts.

"Paquette must have been hell for you," he said.

"It was very hard sometimes, Tom." Her tone was grave and a little sad.

"My poor darling. And Sam Jordan never once raised a finger to help you in it, did he?"

"I never blamed him," Alice said craftily. "He knew he lacked the capacity for handling people. But you can, Tom. That's one of the things about you which attracted me in the first place. The way you get on with people." She paused, sensing he was weakening without in fact understanding why. "Now look, dearest," she said. "I realise that for you to agree would call for a tremendous sacrifice of principle and very great self-control. But offsetting this you would be your own boss and I'd be there to help you as long as you needed me. And" – stealing one of his clichés – "if after you'd given it a fair crack of the whip you found you couldn't bear it, you could always sell the business on like I did Paquette. And by then things might be better. The Conservatives might be back."

"Yes, you can always sell a going concern," Tom said knowledgeably. "That's quite true."

"Or buy one, I suppose. Rather than starting from scratch? Having to go round looking at premises, ordering machinery, interviewing workers."

"I don't think I'd be very good at that. Interviewing workers. Not women. If it were men, that would be another matter. But Micky, is the time right for it? The sort of gowns you used to make . . . Well, if there is a slump like a lot of people are prophesying there's going to be, who's going to buy them?"

Alice nodded, thoughtfully releasing his hand to brush back a lock of hair the breeze had shifted across her forehead. She smiled ruefully. "You see? You do have a business instinct."

"I suppose," Tom said, as if she had guided him into it, "at the lower . . . What do you call it?"

"Range?"

"Yes, range. A lot of people will have to be shifting down into it. The lower range. If things get very tight. As they're going to. Yes, if one was going into that sort of business now it would certainly be important to choose the range of one's operations carefully. Well, it needs a lot of thought but I won't be dog in the manger and dismiss the idea out of hand."

It was a plain request that she drop the subject. Alice had no objections – she knew she'd won.

"We shouldn't be talking business, Tom," she said. "Not on such a lovely day."

"No." He felt the quickening of his heartbeat. "I want to come and lie beside you."

"But there isn't room."

"How much do we need? Lying side by side?"

Alice got the point. But it seemed a strange, uncomfortable and unnecessarily difficult thing to do – to have sex with your husband in a punt.

Eight

1

'As a mark of appreciation of their many years of service' the Eastern Telegraph Company threw a farewell dinner to all the departing members of its staff. As befitted an occasion which marked the abrupt termination of the careers of several scores of men who had assumed they would remain with the company for the whole of their working lives, no expense was spared, with a City Livery Hall hired and full fig – tails, no less – the order of the day.

Having at last persuaded Tom to invest his thousand pounds – or at least as she assumed his thousand pounds – sweetener in a business which she would control, Alice had been instinctively ill at ease about this final get-together. The all-important cheques had been enclosed with the final salary payments on the day previous to the dinner and she would dearly have had it that his arrival home with what Tom joyfully dubbed his 'loot' would have signalled a final break with the men who had so helped to shape his life since Porthcurno. With every passing day she had been haunted by the fear one of them might persuade him to change his mind, the more so as there had naturally been innumerable discussions between those being paid off as how best to use their compensation money and any number of suggestions put forward, some sensible enough, some quite hare-brained.

"Now you're not going to get talked this evening into losing any of that money in some madcap scheme, Tom, are you?" she challenged him.

"Have no fear, Micky," he reassured her gravely. "I've promised to go in with you in the gown business and I won't let you down. My word's my bond."

"I think it's quite absurd having it at all," she objected, hoping against hope that even at this eleventh hour she might dissuade him from going and putting her cup down on the table with exaggerated firmness to underline the point. "It's no different from a lot of boys just leaving school having a party, exchanging addresses and swearing eternal allegiance. And then never meeting each other again! And what'll you do when you get there? Spend the evening swapping smutty jokes, singing bawdy songs and drinking yourselves silly." And, putting her hand on his across the table, "Oh, Tom, do you have to go? We've been getting on so well lately."

As he was intended to, Tom misunderstood her motives. Being persuaded to pool his resources and go into the 'rag trade' with her had given him a purpose in life he had desperately needed. Aware that the men he drank with were hangers-on who would drop him the moment he stopped buying rounds of drinks, and of a sudden seeing himself in the role of a man of affairs, he had abruptly ceased going to the Highbury Barn and in a mood of tremendous altruism promised Alice never to drink again – a promise thus far religiously kept.

"You're worried, aren't you, Micky," he said gravely, "that I'll come off the wagon. I won't, I give you my solemn word. I've learnt my lesson. I'm never going to be a beast to you again."

She did not doubt his sincerity, only his resolve. But she dared not push him further. "You're very kind to me," she said.

"I love you."

"Yes, I know you do." How strange it was, she thought;

she could have been talking to Sam. Was there something the matter with her that she could not even lie and say: 'I love you too'? So few words which would have meant so much to him. But she couldn't say them and pressed his hand instead. "I know you do," she said again. And then, with a smile: "More tea?"

"Please."

While she poured, Tom started buttering toast. "By the way, Micky," he said, "it isn't going to be like you seem to think, at all. This evening, I mean . . . Do you mind passing the marmalade? . . . In fact it's going to be quite an important evening."

"Oh?" An alarm bell rang.

"The marmalade," Tom reminded her. "Thank you." He began spreading it on his toast. "No. We're going to pool ideas and lay down guidelines for assisting any of the chaps who can't get themselves reorganised. Sort of insurance policy, you know."

Alice disliked the sound of this. "You never told me about this before."

"Didn't think you'd be interested, Micky," he mumbled through a mouthful.

"Isn't it going to take all the fun out of it – turning it into . . . well, a sort of conference?" she suggested carefully.

"Lord, no. We'll soon get that part of the evening over."

Although conscious it was dangerous to repeat earlier pleas Alice could not entirely succeed.

"Well I know you're far too sensible and clear-thinking to let anyone bamboozle you into parting with any of your hard-earned compensation money," she compromised.

He chuckled.

"Too true, Micky," he replied with gusto. "What I have, I hold!"

If Alice hadn't known him better, her mind would have been

finally put at rest; as it was she could hardly remember an evening which had dragged by so slowly. There were so many things which she could have been doing. There was a dress she was in the middle of making and some mending to be done, socks to be darned, a skirt hem needing taking up – but she could settle to none of it. She had a pile of fashion magazines she had intended to study – but found herself quite unable to concentrate and turned over page after page only to realise she was registering nothing. She played through their half a dozen records on the gramophone and wished they'd got the wireless they'd talked of buying. It was a golden opportunity to write some overdue letters and she prepared to do so, getting out paper and envelopes, a pen and a bottle of ink, and sitting at the dining table. She thought first of writing to Dessy and Thady but she couldn't think of anything to say that would interest them and in any case they'd be home in a fortnight's time; and when she considered instead writing to her mother to break the news that she would soon be going back into business, it seemed too much like tempting fate. So she put it all away again.

She was only too well aware that the reason for her restlessness was her fear of what could be happening at this very moment in some City Livery Hall; at what might be being hatched among the long tables of men forgetting the discomfort of stiff white shirts and marcella waistcoats in an orgy of drinking, back slapping and maudlin reminiscing.

Try as she might she could not shake off a growing sense of foreboding. She could turn her thoughts in no other direction but the awful prospect facing them if Tom's gratuity was denied her. She paced the rooms, stared from the windows back and front, made herself cups of tea and left them scummed, undrunk. It was the one, the only lifeline left to her. If it *was* denied to her, to whom could she turn for help?

So the hours dragged slowly by. She made herself a sandwich and left most of it uneaten. Listened to the sounds echoing up from the tenants down below. Music from the Warburtons, Mr Jones using the communal lavatory, the front door slamming. The house fell silent. It was midnight, one o'clock, two o'clock – and still Tom hadn't returned. She took herself to bed and at last, out of the sheer exhaustion of the mental strain of the past half dozen hours and more, drifted into uneasy sleep.

The front door slamming roused her. She was at once wide awake. It could only be Tom as late as this. Unless it was that actor, Lancelot Carrington, who was often very late returning. No. She could hear footsteps mounting the stairs. She sat up in bed, concentrating, listening intently, trying to judge by the sound of them what sort of state he would be in. And her heart turned over in dismay.

He came into the bedroom. She saw at once that he was drunk. His face was flushed and glistening, his hair flattened by sweat, his white bow tie stained red with wine, poorly retied and exposing his collar stud, his tailcoat streaked with cigar and cigarette ash, his glacé leather evening shoes badly scratched.

Anger welled up inside her. This was the man who at the very last moment before he got into the taxi cab had *vowed on his honour* to come home sober. She hadn't expected him not to have a drink or two, had realised that to stay teetotal through the whole long evening resisting the joshing and incitement of friends called for a superhuman effort of will of which he was incapable – but surely he could at least on this one occasion, after all his promises and protestations of love, have had *some* self-control.

Inflamed by anger and a sense of utter helplessness her temper urged her to rail at him, to take him to task for his broken promises, to belittle him for his weakness. Only the instinct of self-preservation held her back. If she gave vent to her feelings he would defend himself in the way he always did, by shouting her down, by rampaging around the room, slamming doors, crashing his fist down on her dressing table, even assaulting her. He would become the very man he had vowed never to be again, a man who made her wonder when she looked at him how she could not have seen that within the easy-going, hail-fellow-well-met, universally popular, adoring swain, lurked a bully, petty tyrant, brute. She was afraid of him when he was in these violent moods, but afraid only physically, not mentally. She would stand up to him while he struck her once, or perhaps twice, before the realisation of what he was doing got through to him and he lacked the courage to continue and escaped from his shame into hectoring and stupid clichés then took himself off to somewhere, slamming the door behind him.

Tomorrow would come, leading either into a redefining of his manhood, characterised by statements of a man's right to live his life the way he chose, untied to women's apron strings – which was no more than an excuse to head for the pub at opening time – or a profuse explanation of the pressures that caused him to fall from grace and a renewed undertaking to fight it down and be worthy of the woman he loved. All that would be as it would be and only delay the answer to the question burning her lips and perhaps endanger what was, hopefully, still not at risk.

And so she swallowed her pride, controlled her anger and, forcing a welcoming smile, said simply: "Was it a good evening, Tom?"

The relief on his smudged face was almost pitiful. "Splendid," he slurred, a glint of eagerness moderating the pig-like look his eyes always took on when he was in drink. "Got myself a job."

Alice sat bolt upright. "You did what?"

"Surprised you, eh?"

Alice was aware that in an instant his whole manner had changed. When he came into the room he had been defensive, prickly, primed for confrontation; now, in the twinkling of an eye, reassured by her friendly, neutral question, he was all good humour and disburdened of anxiety.

"Yes, it does," she answered, watching him very closely. "What sort of job, Tom?"

"Book selector!" He said it with pride.

"Book selector? What does that mean?"

"Means that's my responsibility. Sole responsibility." He banged his fist down on her dressing table near which he was now standing, not angrily but triumphantly, and the silver-topped bottles – which, in a crocodile leather case, had been one of Sam's wedding presents – shivered and a tall one fell.

He stood it up again. "'S alright. Thick glass. No damage."

"Your responsibility to do what, Tom?" Alice asked as evenly as her reborn anxiety allowed.

"To choose the books. For the libraries. Harry Reddington-Quarmby's thing."

Harry Reddington-Quarmby's thing! Twopenny lending libraries! Her worst fears resurfaced. Oh no, she begged, please God let that be the whole of it! With a superhuman effort she schooled herself to be calm, to show interest without fear.

She had met Reddington-Quarmby several times when watching Tom play rugger for the Exiles, or at the dances afterwards. He was Club Secretary: arranged the matches, picked the teams, a tireless organiser who never played – why, she hadn't understood, for he was a huge man who would have been, she imagined, invaluable in the ruck. She visualised him now. Tall, six feet four or more, and broad with a mass of flowing Lloyd George hair, unflawed pink skin, a large, beaky nose, and a manner of irrepressible bonhomie – a manner she suspected he'd been at great pains to cultivate. It had always been there: the pipe and the big smile and the belly laugh. She had thought him something of a buffoon, but harmless; now, suddenly, she scented danger.

Of all the schemes bandied around Electra House which

Tom had reported back to her, it had been Harry Reddington-Quarmby's idea of opening a chain of private lending libraries in opposition to the Public Libraries which had worried her most because she had been forced to admit that, if properly managed, it held out reasonable possibilities. She had known he had been going round trying to persuade some of the others to come in with him and had cudgelled her brain – and even been to several public libraries to gather ammunition – to assemble arguments against its chances of success. She *had* believed that Tom had been convinced by them.

"Oh, that twopenny library thing?" she said disparagingly, wondering how she was managing to stay so superficially calm while everything within was at boiling point. "And you're going to select the books. How much is Quarmby" – she decided that from now on she was going to drop the hyphen and the rest of it – "going to pay you?"

"No question of salary, Micky!" He was so jovial now that she couldn't help but believe that he was still under the influence of Quarmby's exhibitionism. "We get our kick-backs out of profit."

Her heart went cold. There was no need really to question him any further. The thousand pounds was lost to her immediately – and lost, before long, she suspected, to both of them.

"Out of profit," she said dully. And turning away, laid her head back on the pillow and stared at the ceiling. She felt drained of vitality – unable to summon up enough energy to round on him for all that there was now nothing to be lost in at least having the satisfaction of telling him exactly what she thought of him. "Assuming there is a profit." And, still not looking at him, "You've been talked into investing your thousand into it, haven't you?"

"Not all," he answered, surprising her. "Alan Sac . . . Sac . . . Sachs thought we ought to limit our investments."

She sat up again to find him sitting on the end of the bed, struggling to loosen the knot of his soiled bow tie.

"To how much?" she asked with a glimmer of hope.

"Five hundred per head."

"Per head. How many idiots like you has Quarmby bamboozled into giving him money?"

"We're not giving him our money." He was highly indignant. "'S not like that at all. 'S a straightforward business invest . . . investment. Got the contract here." He started patting his tailcoat, looking for it.

"You've got the contract!" Alice said disbelievingly. "You mean Quarmby brought them with him to the dinner!"

He stopped looking for the contract as if he'd forgotten it. "Right. Very sensible fellow, Harry Quarmby."

Alice saw it all as clearly as if she had attended the dinner. Quarmby had arrived with a batch of blank contracts to be signed by those who'd already agreed to go in with him and with one or two spare ones for those he hoped to be able to rope in at the last minute.

"And you can't back out now?"

He shook his head. "All signed, sealed and delivered. Anyway, wouldn't if I could. My word's my bond, you know." He had finally got the bow tie undone and was pulling at the end of his starched wing-collar to free it from the stud.

"That's what you said to me."

He had managed to pull one end of the collar free and it flew up almost to his ear. He desisted with its fellow to say: "Know I did, old girl. But this is a golden opportunity. Going to make us rich." He chuckled. "As Croesus. Millions and millions of people wanting to read. An' all fed up with the stuffy public libraries—"

"But Tom," she interrupted angrily. "You agreed with me. We talked about lending libraries . . ."

"Know I did, old girl," he said, apparently unaware he had repeated himself. "An' you had some good points. Matter 'f fact I put them to this Sachs fellow."

"Who's he?" Alice demanded, uninterested in how her arguments had apparently been shot down in flames.

"Eastern director."

"A director of the Eastern Telegraph Company!?"

"That's right."

"What was he doing at your dinner?"

Tom pulled the other tab of the collar free and began to attack the stud itself.

"Top table," he said. "With the nobs. Was there when we arrived to welcome us with a sherry. Didn't have one, Micky. Said no. Said no to the wine too. Was all right until the loving cup went round. Well, couldn't do much about that, could I? Fellow hands you this cup filled with wine with a towel hanging from it. Well, you can't say no, can you? Breaks the chain. Bad luck all round if you do that."

Alice could not have cared less at what stage Tom had been coerced into breaking his pledge. All that mattered was that he had done so – and had from that moment been putty in Quarmby's hands. Her instincts told her that this had all been carefully engineered and that Quarmby was not alone in it. That this Sachs had to be involved as well.

"This man Sachs," she probed. "Is he investing in this lending library thing?"

"Not 'xactly." He had difficulty with the word. "But he's promised to up the ante if we need more money."

"That's very generous of him."

Tom missed the irony. "Generous fellow." He had got the collar stud undone exposing a red weal below his Adam's apple where a collar at least one size too small had pressed it in. With an exhalation of breath which directed drink fumes all over Alice, he sat down so heavily on the end of the bed as to make it creak alarmingly and, bending, started to attack his shoes.

Alice realised that in his present state there was not much more she was going to get out of him. By the time he'd got his clothes off, if the drink in him hadn't made him amorously disposed, which as often as not it did, he'd be ready for sleep and in two minutes snoring his head off.

Her instincts told her there was more to know about this lending library business, probably more to know than Tom even when sober could tell her. In running Paquette, she had had to hold her own amongst hard-bitten businessmen and women who had the skill to camouflage their ulterior motives under various fronts amongst which had been included both apparent uninterest and generosity. She suspected that this mysterious Sachs was such a man. Why else should a one-time director of a company which had ceased to exist not merely bother to waste an evening on a bunch of one-time underlings but take it on himself to advise them how to spend, or not to spend, their money?

She resolved that tomorrow she would look more deeply into this, discuss it with the lawyer, Weldon, and maybe even seek out Messrs Harold Reddington-Quarmby and Alan Sachs. In the meantime there was still the other half of Tom's gratuity. Five hundred pounds.

"Tom," she said to his back.

"Uhm?" He was unlacing a shoe.

"The other five hundred pounds. You're in no way committed to investing that, as well, are you?"

He looked round over his shoulder, collar adrift, end of soiled bow tie hanging over ash-smeared silk lapels, a lick of hair over a sweat-beaded forehead. "Haven't got five hundred, Micky, anyway," he said – and went back to attacking his shoes.

Whether the admission simply slipped out of a drink-befuddled brain, or cunning suggested that as he was obviously in the doghouse he might as well get it all over in one fell swoop, Alice was never to know.

"You must have!" she cried. "You got a thousand yesterday and if you're only committed to five hundred in this . . .

this ridiculous thing Quarmby and this man Sachs have so obviously cooked up between them . . ."

He levered off a shoe and hurled it accurately into the open wardrobe. "Good shot, Fenwick!"

"Did you hear what I said?"

"Heard what you said." He was attacking the second shoe. "Never was a thousand, Micky," he said to it. "There was what was left after paying off the Tappenden business. Bank nipped that off at source when I paid it in."

"But you were paying that off as you went along."

"Stopped doing that when I knew I was going to get the thousand." He got off the second shoe and threw it after its fellow and, standing up, began the business of more serious undressing.

"So how much is left?"

"Can't say offhand. Hundred or two I s'pose."

"A hundred or two!"

He waved a casual hand dismissing such petty considerations. "There were other things." He forced out a belch. "Manners!" He took a hanger from the wardrobe and was about to hang his tailcoat on it when he saw the ash greying the front. He made an ineffectual pass of his hand to brush it off, missing the coat by inches. "Uh! See to it in the morning. Plenny of time now I don't have to go to the Eastern." He started to undo the pearl buttons on his marcella waistcoat which was stained red as well.

"Tom!" Alice shrieked, anger mounting in spite of all her good intentions. "Listen to me! And answer me!"

He paused, mouth open. "Wassit?"

"How can you only have a hundred or two? It wasn't three hundred you still owed over that Tappenden business. It was only fifty or sixty. We worked it out. Together."

Tom waved his hand again. "Well, there were a few more bills. Like . . . well, sometimes I was a bit short and old Leonard at the Barn obliged."

The full horror of the situation struck home. He had been cashing cheques in pubs against the security of the Eastern pay-off. There was nothing left. Or nothing of consequence. A hundred or two maybe – more likely less. For all practical purposes the money on which they were to rebuild their finances had all gone: in drink and a crackpot scheme which would take years to produce an income if it ever produced one at all.

She was on her own. Apart from companionship in those periods when he was behaving like a reasonable human being. Tom Fenwick had nothing at all to offer her. Whatever was to be achieved through the remainder of her life depended on herself and on herself alone. With a sweeping gesture she threw back the bedcovers, swivelled her feet to the floor and reached for her dressing gown hanging on a hook behind the door.

"Where are you going, Micky?" Tom, pausing in taking off his stiff shirt, demanded in a surprised and disappointed tone.

"To Dessy's room."

"But . . . No, don't go." There was plaintive appeal in his voice for all that he looked anything but romantic with his trousers held up by braces, the stiff shirt half opened and the collar ends at his ears. "I want to make love to you. I've been thinking about it all the way home."

"Well, you can go on thinking."

Shoving her feet into the slippers beside the bed, she heard him staggering to his feet and lifting her head she saw him standing over her, clenched fist raised. His face only inches from hers was suffused with rage, his eyes bloodshot, glaring. She was not shocked. She had seen this happen before. This sudden metamorphosis which turned a warm and reasonable human being into a frightening brute. "Now you hear me, woman!" he yelled in a voice which must surely have woken the Warburtons on the floor below. "This is my house and what I say in it goes! A man has rights!"

A waft of brandy encompassed her and disgust of him conquered fear.

"A man has rights only when he's earned them, which you haven't; and it's not a house, it's an attic flat which I've furnished and you pay rent for!" she retorted with crucifying contempt. "You stink of drink and if you think I'm going to have you slobbering over me tonight, then you've got another guess coming. I'm going to go and sleep in Dessy's room and I warn you, Tom – if you come and bother me in any way, then in the morning I shall leave you and not come back."

And she left him, closing the door behind her.

Nine

Joseph Mott's office at the corner of Chancery Lane and Holborn was a tomb stacked up with office furniture to its very entrance. There were desks, chairs, wire racks, storage files, chests, tables, cabinets and stools, all making their own corridors which led to other desks, chairs, wire racks, storage files, chests, tables, cabinets and stools. And amongst all these were second-hand typewriters by the hundred with no special place of residence for any of them but all shoved in here and there and everywhere, wherever one of them would fit. They were poked between the desks, sat upon the chairs, propped against the storage files, stacked upon the cabinets, balanced on the stools. They had a strange appearance, did these second-hand typewriters, ten thousand tin shanks of arms, ten thousand oily keys all woolly with London dust. They had no life, only names: Remington, Royal, Reliant; no life, and yet they seemed to brood. You could imagine them at night when silence had descended on the City whispering to each other from their hideyholes, thinly chattering the secrets they had been forced to put on paper: the threats, the pleas, the hopes, the gloats, the triumphs, the despairs. They were slaves thrown aside until a new master would come to buy them – you felt the coldness in them and the hate.

"This way, madam, if you please," a clearly awed, pimply young office boy directed an Alice whose perfume brought romance and a different way of living into the dusty den in which he worked; an Alice who was in her best, shriekingly up-to-date finery: a day dress and matching jacket with the waist up at the normal waist position instead of at the hips and a loose, calf-length, swinging pleated skirt – and because with her longer hair it was no longer possible to wear a cloche, she wore with it a soft hat, trimmed with a band of the same material, pulled down over one eye. It was a brand new outfit bought with calculated extravagance only a day or two before. If I am going to try to get back into business, she had reasoned, I can only do so by getting someone to back me and the only hope I have of achieving that is to present myself to the world as a successful woman not just up to date but ahead of fashion.

And, she had discovered, there was more, far more to it than that. The moment she spun in front of her bedroom mirror to enjoy the effect of the pleated skirt twirling out, she felt a resurgence of the self-confidence she had known in the days of Belmont when Paquette was prospering and no thought of leaving Sam for Tom had crossed her mind.

She followed the boy along a wider passage between the walls of merchandise and came upon Joseph crouched at a chipped and cluttered desk amid the cave of furniture which threw weird bars of shadows into a pool of light from the green-shaded dusty bulb underneath which he worked. He looked, she decided, like a frog caught glinting in some tenebrous cranny, gobbling up its prey. Either he had not heard her coming or was pretending not to have heard it.

Her arm caught some small thing, a paperweight, or a seal perhaps, sent it skittering down a desk front, clattering amongst some chairs, dying on the floor and he looked up.

"Alice!" His eyes roved over her. "But how wonderful you look!" he cried. "Like something out of Vogue itself! I was going to take you to lunch at Slaters but looking like you do it can only be the Crébillion."

"I didn't," said Alice, with a fluttering in her heart at the thought of actually going to the Crébillion which the magazines had recently voted as London's most chic lunchtime restaurant, "ask you to see me with the idea of being taken out to lunch."

"You merely chose the appropriate time for calling."

"I chose the time because you told me Sam wouldn't be here then."

"And you chose the dress you are wearing because it was the only little thing you had which was suitable for a private tête-à-tête in a dusty City office crammed with rusty typewriters. Oh, come now, Alice, we've known each other far too long."

"Aren't you going to ask me why I wanted to see you?"

"My dear Alice, I know exactly why you want to see me. But this is a very special occasion which we ought not to spoil one moment earlier than we have to." He thumped a brass desk bell which sent a clear summons ringing through the curious warehouse. As if by magic, the office boy appeared.

"Henry," Joseph, clearly in splendid humour, chortled. "Summon a taxi cab!"

"Yes, sir."

"Now," said Joseph, "while we are waiting, let me see if I can find you a chair." He got to his feet and looked about him. "Ah! Here we are!" He scraped the chair in question an inch or two nearer and opening a drawer in his desk pulled out a yellow cloth and ostentatiously dusted it off. Alice wondered if this was the chair on which Sam spent all his time when not actually out tramping the City streets selling Joseph's typewriters.

"Please," said Joseph, beaming.

Alice sat, crossed her legs with careful deliberation, and, having arranged the folds of her skirt, rested her hands one on top of the other on her thigh and raised her head challengingly. "Have you told Sam I was coming in to see you?"

"No."

"And will you tell him later that I did?"

"Would you mind?"

"I don't suppose I have any choice." And, when he did not respond, "It's rather odd, but I haven't run across him lately."

"No, you wouldn't."

There was meaning in it but the mocking eyes behind the big round glasses gave nothing away.

"If I have to discover the significance of that remark, I have to ask for it, don't I?" Alice said.

"Oh, it's very simple. Samuel is no longer living in Woodstock Hotel."

"He isn't?"

"No. He's got a house farther up Highbury New Park. Number one-seven-six."

"You love forcing people to to be supplicants, don't you, Joseph," Alice said, breaking the silence which followed this remarkable statement. "It gives you a sense of power, I suppose. But all right, I won't be proud. Tell me why."

"He's got a new idea." He burst into one of his explosions of merriment. Alice knew that in moments the glasses would be off, a handkerchief would appear and Joseph would be wiping his eyes. "A bridge club!"

"A what?"

"A bridge club!" The glasses were off. The handkerchief had appeared. "A place where people can gather together to play contract bridge. Have you ever heard of anything so bizarre? He thinks that people will come and pay what he calls 'table money' and that will cover the cost of providing them with cups of tea and biscuits. Oh, dear!" He wiped his eyes.

"Oh," said Alice. And, after a moment's thought: "He's not doing it to make money then?"

"Now when was Samuel interested in making money?"

"There was a time," said Alice, stung.

"Ah, yes. The jute days." He pocketed the handkerchief and replaced his gold-rimmed spectacles. It was if she had recalled to his mind something long forgotten.

"So what's he doing? Renting this house?"

"Oh, no. He's a landlord, not a tenant. He's letting off rooms to all manner of strange people. Poles. Czechs. Armenians. Even a Chinaman, I'm told."

Alice wondered how much was truth, how much to satisfy Joseph Mott's devious brand of humour.

"You mean he owns it?" she said.

"Even the top attic floor."

Alice ignored the barb. "Did his mother die and leave him something after all?"

"Oh, no. She's still alive and living in Crogellan House. No, I bought it for him."

"*You* bought it? *Gave* it to him?" She could not believe it.

"Well, I couldn't have him go on living in that dreadful Woodstock place, could I?"

The office boy materialised. "Taxi's here, sir."

"Thank you, Henry, you were very quick!" Joseph said and, amazingly, felt in his pocket, withdrew a half crown and gave it to the boy, who gazed at it in open-mouthed astonishment – as well he might considering it probably represented half his weekly wages. "Well, take it, Henry," Joseph said jovially. "Before I change my mind." And, rising to his feet, "Come, Alice." And, guiding her by her arm, he led her out.

"You would never have bought Sam that house if we hadn't split up, would you, Joseph?" They were in the taxi and heading down Chancery Lane.

"Never."

"You'd have let him see his life out in Belmont Hotel spending all his waking time when he wasn't working for you in that dreadful little bridge room."

"It was where he liked best to be."

"So long as we were living in Belmont."

"Since you ask the question, yes."

"I didn't say it as a question."

"Then I accept it as a statement. Yes."

"If you'd given him this house when we lost our money, we might still be together, mightn't we?"

"Yes, you probably would be."

"You worked it out, didn't you?" Her tone was bitter. "Took into account all the factors. The difference in our backgrounds. The fact that Sam was heading for *middle* age and Belmont was chock full of young people of *my* age. You calculated that sooner or later a Tom Fenwick would come along and free Sam for you."

"How very well analysed. And how you've come along. I'm full of admiration."

"You don't admire me. You loathe the sight of me. You always have."

He laughed – a laugh very different from his normal laugh. A laugh against himself. "Loathe the sight of you? Good heavens, where on earth did you get that idea from? Apart from invariably being a delight to look at, I have always admired you. I admired you from the very first moment I laid eyes upon you. I knew that Samuel had won himself a jewel beyond compare."

"Oh, don't talk such nonsense!" Alice snapped irritably. "The first time you saw me was on the day Sam and I got married because even though you were going to be his best man, he wouldn't let me meet you before. I think he was afraid of what you'd have to say about me and my family. That I was an ignorant, naïve, half-educated teenager and my father was a Liverpudlian railway ticket collector and he would be marrying out of his class and it couldn't possibly work!"

"Which of course it couldn't," Joseph said. "But not for any of those reasons."

A top-hatted doorman in beige livery opened the taxi door and ushered her out like royalty.

"I will wait for you here in the foyer," Joseph said.

She took this as an instruction to visit the ladies' cloakroom and, although she had no need, dutifully did so, goggled a little at the opulence of it, and while powdering her face and touching up her lips spent a full five minutes preparing her mind for lunching in a place which she knew was patronised by high society. Returning, she was guided by Joseph to a small table in a dark and heavily panelled restaurant ante-room which was hung with heavy swagged burgundy drapes and projected an undeniably intimate, masculine and almost claustrophobic atmosphere from which the busy world of the West End was entirely banished. Beside the table to which Joseph led her was an ice bucket and champagne.

A waiter materialised at once, deftly uncorked the bottle, poured two glasses, bowed and withdrew. Alice noticed the wine was pink – a new discovery.

"*Sante*!" said Joseph, raising his glass.

Alice, hiding her surprise at this remarkable indulgence on Joseph's part, raised her own, echoed *Santé*!, drank a little wine and immediately posed one of the questions she had prepared in the cloakroom: "Does it mean anything? Crébillion?"

"It means," said Joseph, "that the owner, who is not a Frenchman but a Cypriot named Boghaz, set his stall out for a theatrical clientèle. Seven Dials is handy for Shaftesbury Avenue and Crébillion was a contemporary of Voltaire if not in quite the same class. He was, Crébillion, a bloodthirsty dramatist whose characters specialised in either killing their sons or drinking their gore – hence the Grand Guignol atmosphere."

"I didn't know," said Alice, genuinely impressed, "that you had such an interest in the theatre."

"Nor have I," gurgled Joseph. "But if you use a restaurant for entertaining you have to read it up so as to appear a cognoscente."

"You come here often?"

"Not infrequently."

"It helps sell your typewriters?" said Alice disbelievingly.

"No," Joseph said. "Not my typewriters."

"Have you ever bought Sam lunch or dinner here?"

He chuckled merrily. "No. With his socialist tendencies he would thoroughly disapprove of it."

The head waiter appeared with two massive menus. "Good morning, Mr Mott." His face wore the comfortable smile of one greeting a valued customer and his manner exuded the familiarity of one of consequence to another.

"Good morning, Ivor." Joseph answered, equally at ease. And, to Alice: "Shall we get the tiresome business of ordering our lunch over first and then we can carry on with our discussion without being interrupted?" He signalled to Ivor to pass one of the menus to her. She glanced at it only long enough to note that none of the items on it carried prices, then, again using her five minutes' planning purposefully, shook her head, dismissing the menu out of hand. "I would like," she said (emulating Sam's sister at an important lunch at the Montpelier in Dean Street many years before at which, out of her depth as to decide what to order, she had ordered the same as Hetty had), "grilled sole with a green salad and thin brown bread and butter."

"What a splendid notion," Joseph chuckled. "I will have the same." And, to the head waiter: "And I think we will start with prosciutto and melon. But please do not call us to the table until . . ." He glanced at his watch. "Until one thirty. And tell Felix we will have the Mersault. He knows the one I like."

Ivor bowed with just the correct degree of obsequiousness and withdrew. Alice, meanwhile, looking around her, noticed with a frisson of delight that at the very next table to theirs in this sombre ante-room was Delysia Shelley who had the lead in 'Story at Twilight' which had opened in Shaftesbury Avenue a few days before and had had rave reviews. She was in a party of six, four men and another woman. Delysia Shelley was dramatic-looking with ashen skin, high cheekbones, a jutting jaw and wide-set, staring, olive-coloured eyes which gave the impression of focusing on nothing nearer than the far wall of the restaurant. The second woman had baggy, almond-shaped, almost oriental eyes in a puffy face. The men were unremarkable except for one of them who was a swarthy, South American hunchback. All were treating Delysia Shelley with enormous respect, hanging on to her every word, their eyes for no one else.

"You know who she is?" Joseph asked, catching her unawares.

"Yes. Delysia Shelley. I wonder who the others are."

"The woman with her is her agent. The gnome is what is known as an angel – he backs West End plays – and the others are to do with the current play she's in."

"*Story at Twilight.* Do you know them or something?"

He laughed as if she had said something droll. "No. I asked Ivor while I was waiting for you in the foyer."

Alice's eyes roved further, hoping to spot a Noel Coward or a Jack Buchanan perhaps, but Joseph brought her smartly back to earth.

"And how is little Dessy?"

This was awkward inasmuch as it was largely on account of Desmond and Thady that Alice had stilled compunction and swallowed pride and she had intended to steer the conversation less directly round to them.

"Oh, he's fine."

"And little Joseph?"

'Joseph' was Thady. He had been christened Joseph as a sop to Mott – who had agreed to be his godfather – in the hope that he, and Desmond, would not be forgotten when Mott came to write his will. The 'Joseph' had long since been abandoned – and its abandonment never overlooked by Mott.

"Yes," Alice said, refusing the bait. "He's well too."

"They'll be breaking up for their summer holidays soon."

"In a few days' time." Oh, what was the point? She'd have to get round to it sooner or later. "It was as much about them as anything else that I wanted to see you." And, as he nodded his balding head benignly: "Tom's lost his job."

He startled her. "Yes, I know."

"How do you know?" she challenged him.

He chuckled. "My dear Alice, surely you would not expect me not to keep myself up to date in any matter with which my godchild was concerned? No, I have assiduously followed the affairs of the Eastern Telegraph Company since that little dinner we had at Belmont. You, Samuel, Fenwick and myself. Fenwick, you'll remember, was waxing lyrically about the integrity of the firm he was working for and trying to convince us it was one of the many businesses which were being run honestly and squarely. Honestly and squarely – those were his words, not mine. I suggested, if you recall, that if he was correct then it would not be long before it was gobbled up by a predator. Well, naturally, having made such a prognostication, I have since been following its affairs. You would surely not have expected me to do anything else, would you?"

"No," said Alice bitterly. "I wouldn't."

"Oh, come now," Joseph said jovially. "Surely it is in any case better that I should have acquainted myself of the situation before we met. You have many problems." And, obviously intending to list them: "A husband who has been trained for a very specialised occupation who has been bought off with a bribe of one thousand pounds in cash and two pounds a week for life—"

"You even know the details!" Alice said, horrified.

"Oh, they were not very difficult to ascertain. As I was saying, you have a husband trained for a particular operation and for nothing else whatsoever who has been foolish enough to accept a pittance in return for having his contract broken while you, meanwhile, in order to marry him, have foolishly sold your splendid business. You have two children who for the next ten years or so have to be fed, clothed, housed and educated. We live in difficult times—"

Alice, stung by this accurate assessment of her predicament, interrupted sharply: "You wouldn't think they were difficult times—"

"Sitting here, in a place like this, drinking champagne? Quite so. And, please, Alice, do drink a little more of it. It is very good champagne and with every bubble rising to the surface it is deteriorating. Please!" He picked up his glass and held it towards her as in a toast.

She would willingly have picked up her own and dashed the contents in his face. But where else was there to turn? She had known in advance that even if he was going to help he would first put her through this kind of persecution, just as Dessy and Thady had to endure a pinching before he gave them toys he had bought for them. What was the point of torturing yourself with the shame of it and girding yourself up to face his rudeness, ridicule, sarcasm, insults even, and then at the very first hurdle giving way to anger and exasperation? No. She must steel herself, let him enjoy his 'I told you so's', and suffer his little ironies and the curious form of badinage which seemed to give him so much pleasure, at least until such time as she was *certain* he wasn't going to help. There was no one else.

"It's a Laurent Perrier, Cuveé Rosé Brut," Joseph encouraged her meanwhile. "Rather special, don't you think?"

"So far as I'm concerned it's just champagne," Alice said, switching off from her surroundings. "Except that I didn't know it came in pink as well as yellow." And, having drunk some of it: "Do you always order pink champagne for the ladies you entertain?"

"Yellow!" chortled Joseph. "How splendidly brave you are. The first person I've known who's dared to call champagne anything but golden. As for your question, no, I do not. But for you, my dear Alice, for this special occasion and as a compliment to the elegance of your dress, which in case you have not noticed it has caught everyone's eyes, nothing else would have been appropriate."

Alice got the point. He was prepared to go on with this nonsense indefinitely. The onus was on her to get down to practicalities.

"Yes. Well, it is very nice, but I don't have the opportunity of becoming a champagne connoisseur," she said briskly. "Now, I asked you if you would see me, Joseph, because I wanted your advice on one or two things and then perhaps your help."

Joseph spread his hands a trifle. "Madame, I am at your service."

Alice drank a little more champagne to cover deciding where to start, then put the glass well aside.

"When my husband told me he was going to lose his job and get this compensation money, I was terrified he'd either fritter it away or invest it in some hare-brained scheme as many of the other Eastern men are doing." She paused. "As I expect you know?" He nodded. "Most of what I'd put by from Paquette has gone in buying furniture, paying school fees and heaven knows what else, so I decided I'd lay my hands on Tom's compensation money if I could and use it to start a new Paquette. I managed to persuade him to agree to it – it wasn't easy – and right up to a dinner that was given in some City Livery Hall—"

"The Vintners'."

"Is there any point in my going on at all?"

"Every point," he beamed, and took off his glasses and began to polish them with a silk handkerchief without taking his eyes off hers.

"Well, it seems that until they had reached the stage when most of them had drunk so much sherry and wine and port and brandy as to be incapable of discussing anything sensibly, most of the conversation *was* about this thousand pounds and what they were going to do with it. There were two or three of them with their own pet schemes who were trying to persuade others to come in with them."

"Such as?" His eyes were glinting with, she fancied, genuine interest.

"Oh," she said dismissively. "There was one who wanted to be an on-course bookmaker and another who fancied himself as . . ." She glanced at the adjacent table and saw to her surprise that it had been vacated. "Well, like that man you called a gnome."

"An impresario?" He chuckled. "He might just as well bet his money with the one who's going to be a bookmaker."

"Yes. Well, there was another one who had an idea of starting a chain of lending libraries. Do you think that's equally stupid?"

Joseph replaced the spectacles. "No," he said. "I don't think it's stupid, just difficult."

"Why difficult?"

"Because of the capital required. You've got to rent the premises, staff them, buy the books."

"Yes. Well, this man, who rejoices under the name of Harold Reddington-Quarmby, managed to persuade half a dozen of them to come in with him and he'd brought a few extra contracts with him to the dinner in the hope of persuading one or two more."

"Brought the contracts with him! Oh, ho!"

"That's exactly how I felt. Well, it seems he wasn't getting very far but there was this man Alan Sachs, who used to be a director of the Eastern Telegraph Company, who was there, at the top table, and he made an after-dinner speech reminding them that a thousand pounds was several years' salary, and they must be very careful with it and then of course everyone started asking him what he thought about these various schemes and he damned them all out of hand except for Quarmby's library thing."

"Don't tell me Fenwick fell for it? Signed one of those contracts?"

"Yes."

"Why don't I have the luck to meet more men like your husband when I'm doing business?" He folded both hands on what was now an ample stomach and stared at her as interrogatively as if he really meant the question to be taken seriously. And when she did not reply, shrugged and, removing his hands to his knees, enquired: "And this man Sachs?"

"Sachs?" Alice was puzzled.

"Well, it's very very odd. A director of a company which has ceased to exist attends a dinner—"

"I gather he organised the dinner."

"Ah ha!" cried Joseph triumphantly.

"What d'you mean?" demanded Alice – although she could have answered the question herself.

"Well, it's obvious, isn't it? The man's in cahoots with this Quarmby fellow." He chuckled. "I'm afraid, my dear Alice, it will be a long time before you get any return on that thousand pounds. As for getting it back . . ." He shook his head.

Alice, in an instinct to defend Tom's credibility, objected: "But they're getting very popular, these twopenny lending libraries."

"Just a minute." Joseph reached into his pocket and drew out a letter and a gold fountain pen. "If I were Samuel," he said, "I wouldn't need this, I could do it in my head." He put the letter upside down on the table and started doing calculations on the back of the envelope. When he had finished he said: "Well, there it is. Say there's five fools like Fenwick put their thousands in. Five thousand. There's premises, doing them up, notepaper, equipment and so on leaving – what, for books? Half, say? And you'd be lucky. How many books shall we say? Ten thousand at five shillings each? Twopence to borrow them for a fortnight. Say half out at a time. Works out at two thousand one hundred and sixty pounds a year. And there's rates, staff to pay, postage, telephone, heating, cleaning and book replacement – a lot get simply stolen and not returned. Might be a thousand profit. Might be. But I doubt it. Mightn't even be a profit. And what's Fenwick's share for his thousand pounds if there is that profit? One hundred pounds a year?"

"But," Alice said desperately, "there *are* lending libraries. They must make a profit or they wouldn't be there."

"If every kind of business automatically succeeded we wouldn't need bankruptcy courts."

"You think there's no hope for lending libraries then?"

"I didn't say that. But they have to be long-term projects properly financed. Not pipe dreams put together by men whose only qualification is the ability to tap out and read messages in morse code."

"Then why should this man Sachs go out of his way to approve it?"

Joseph chuckled. "My dear Alice, you're practical enough to answer that yourself."

Alice shook her head and Joseph decided that, delightful though her dress was, it was the hat pulled down over her left eye which gave her the chic she had lacked before.

"I imagine," he said, "that Sachs will wait until Quarmby's lending library is about to fail through lack of capital and then come in with an offer for the shares at a knock-down price."

"But would it be worth his while?"

"Why not? Let's say he buys the first subscribers out at twenty per cent of what they invested. That'll probably be about it. So he's got a five thousand pound investment for one thousand and all the donkey work done by others." He nodded an approving head. "Smart fellow, Sachs."

For some reason the remark rang a bell in Alice's mind. "I don't *believe* you've bought that house for Sam!" she said triumphantly.

"Well, there's a *non sequitur*, if ever I heard one."

"No, it isn't! You've bought it and let Sam rent it off you for a pound a year or something."

He ducked his head respectfully. "What a clever girl you are."

But for all his resumption of his tongue-in-check approach, in that moment Joseph realised that this attractive, exceptionally-turned-out woman had become one seriously to be reckoned with. For all his flippant public treatment of her, he had always secretly respected her for her ability to absorb, her capacity to face adversity and rise above it and her energy, initiative and imagination. But he had viewed her within the confines of what it was imaginable for a pretty girl reared in a cloth-cap background, however quick on the uptake, to achieve. Now he knew that he had been wrong. That, given the support which she had obviously come to seek, there might well be no limits to what she might accomplish. And had she been anyone else she would have had no need to ask for support, he would have offered it.

'What a clever girl you are.' The words meanwhile echoed in Alice's mind. "Do you think so?" she said. And came directly to the point: "Then would you back me in a new business on a properly worked out business footing?"

"No," said Joseph.

It was said so uncompromisingly as to leave her in no doubt that it was useless to pursue it further.

She saw the head waiter approaching – obviously to suggest they went into lunch. She made a decision – if Joseph wasn't going to help in *any* way, she was damned if she was going to sit down and eat prosciutto – whatever that was – with him.

"Desmond and Thady," she said. "I would like your advice on them. About their education!" She was just in time. Ivor was at their table. She looked up at him sharply. "You can tell the chef we will be going in ten minutes from now," she said with intentional curtness. He bowed satisfactorily and withdrew.

"Well, well, well!" said Joseph, grinning.

"Well, well, well, nothing!" she retorted. "About Desmond and Thady. Currently, they're at a small boarding school in Wormley. What we, Tom and I, have to decide is where they go after that."

"There's obviously only one place they can go to. Where their father went. Baylock."

"You think they'd get in? At such short notice?"

"No question. You need only mention who their father is and when they've looked up his scholastic record, they'll jump at having them."

"And of course it's where you went, Joseph, isn't it?"

"Oh, don't mention me. I wouldn't be of the slightest help."

"The only thing is," Alice said, "until such time as either Tom's investment in this library thing starts producing income, or he gets a job that pays enough or I establish another Paquette, we can't afford it." And, baldly, "I suppose, being Thady's godfather, you wouldn't pay *his* fees at least, would you?"

Joseph grinned. "I might pay Desmond's. I might have paid Joseph's. But never Thady's. I do have pride, you know."

It was a fearful, calculated snub. With a huge effort Alice controlled herself and, with eyes blazing with dislike, snapped back: "And so do I!" And, seeing the head waiter hovering in the opening between ante-room and dining room, summoned him peremptorily and, reaching for her handbag, said when he came up: "Will you have someone get me a taxi cab. I won't be lunching after all."

Ivor, showing not the least flicker of surprise, replied: "Of course, madam. It may take a few minutes; there aren't many which arrive as late as this and anyway it has started raining heavily." He bowed and withdrew.

"Bravo!" said Joseph – but she was gratified to see that his normally pasty face was as pink as the champagne in their glasses.

There were a few minutes to fill. She could hardly stand

around in the empty foyer or in the pouring rain outside. If she couldn't find a way of using them, Joseph would. She sought for something casual and unrelated to her reason for contacting him.

"I shan't be bothering you again, Joseph," she said. "But before I go there's one thing I would like to know."

"What's that?"

"What's prosciutto?"

She knew at once from the gleam in his eye that it might have been better to have kept silent.

"Prosciutto," he told her, "is also known as Parma ham."

"Ah." She had heard of Parma ham.

"But that is a misnomer. Properly defined, prosciutto is smoked Italian ham cut wafer thin. A delicacy, my dear Alice, which it never occurred to the redoubtable Mrs Latta to serve in Belmont or that you are ever likely to afford on your share of income from Mr Quarmby's twopenny library. But it is something you should bear in mind ordering when you are setting out to impress others less knowledgeable than yourself."

Stung by the insult, Alice countered: "We evidently have quite different ideas on what it is important to know. You have your business . . ."

"And you have your children." The interruption was too swift not to have been a prepared one. Alice was baffled – but not for long. "But of course you *don't* know them, do you?"

She felt her cheeks flame.

"How could you?" he continued as if this had been an answer. "Before the second one could even walk you incarcerated them in an hotel which saved you the trouble of doing all the normal things a mother does by which she comes to know her children intimately. They stand beside her while she's cooking, watch her make the beds, go shopping with her and all the rest of it – and while she's carrying out these motherly duties they're asking questions and telling her their hopes, their fears, and the little secrets they'd never think of telling a hotel maid or waiter."

"I'm doing those things now! That's why I—" She broke off.

"Why you married Fenwick? Really? Well, let's not go into that; it might take all day and your taxi will be here any moment. As for doing those things now . . . Haven't you got in mind going back into business and keeping them in the boarding school you've already shunted them off to?"

"There's the holidays."

"Did Paquette close for the children's holidays?" He shrugged. "Not that it matters. It's too late now. They've had to find their own design for living, to cope with such mysteries as sex—"

"They're too young for sex to come into it."

"How little you know. And now you've lumbered them with a stepfather whose background, attitudes and character has to be vastly different from their own so it won't be any good their going to him with their little problems, will it? You've two choices, Alice. The first is to pack 'em off to Liverpool. Permanently. After all, they share the same blood and were happier with your parents, and the brothers and sisters you very sensibly never invited to come and visit you down here, than they ever were in Belmont."

"And the second choice?" said Alice coldly.

"The second choice is to rid yourself of Fenwick. He's a millstone round your neck who will drag you down into depths from which even you with all your energy, courage and determination will be unable to rise again. My dear Alice, you have qualities vouchsafed to very few women and you mustn't waste them. Free yourself from Fenwick, go back into business, make it your life and organise your children in such a way that they will not interfere with your career. It is the only hope left in life for you and, very possibly, the only hope for Desmond and Thady too."

"Well, there's one thing certain," Alice snapped. "It's no good either of them looking to you for help!"

He chuckled and held up a hand on which the diamond ring he had bought from Alice when the catastrophe of Sam's bankruptcy occurred glittered coldly. "My dear Alice," he said, "I wouldn't be too sure of that. The time may very well come when they feel they need someone to turn to for advice. And who better a person for them to turn to than their father's oldest friend?"

Ten

1

It is difficult to conceive any meeting place more conducive to illuminating a family's way of life than a shared lavatory. Whether on the throne or in the tub, Iaan Jones found himself times without number pressurised by urgent tappings on the door and plaintive pleas from Desmond or Thady that their requirements were not such as could be met by piddling down the sloping mansard roof (which soon became their almost exclusive method of urinating), by requests from Alice couched in firm but apologetic terms and by Tom, when, according to his state of intoxication, communicated anything from a courteous: "You'll let me know, old man, when you're out, won't you?" to a slurred: "For God's sake, do you have to hog the bloody place!?"

And there were of course the occasions when both Jones and one of the Fenwicks arrived together or met when arriving and vacating coincided, necessitating brief salutations accompanied by a probable reference to the weather. Such meetings being at any time of the day or night, Jones ran across them blazered and flannelled, in sober office suiting, in workaday skirt and jumper, dressed to kill for dance or theatre, in nightdress or pyjamas, in dressing gown and even underpants. He saw them in a frantic hurry, just stumbled out of bed tousle-haired, unshaven or devoid of make-up; he saw them crisply brushed and combed, bay-rummed and perfumed.

He came to know them in varied moods: Desmond and Thady

excited at the prospect of some promised diversion or bored out of their minds after being left to fend for themselves in a half-furnished flat with only a gramophone and half a dozen records for entertainment; Alice in a practical state of mind just off to Highbury Barn to do some shopping or pale and harassed after a sleepless night; Tom, tennis grip in hand, genial and animated or redolent of drink, shifty-eyed, quarrelsome and guilty. And hearing raised voices and the slamming of doors he put it all together and made a fair judgement of what life must be like for the two young boys in the floors above him.

He was a cheerful roly-poly of a man of about five feet six, with a very round but fearfully damaged face, an unparted mop of very thick black hair and a parrot's beak of a nose, who travelled in printed stationery, his absurdly vast territory roughly extending northwards to Highgate, southwards to the Thames, eastwards to Hackney Marshes and westwards to Paddington. In other words the firm for whom he worked hadn't actually allocated an area to him – he could go wherever he chose and was limited solely by his energy and his capacity for shrugging off rejections and, for all his rather disturbing appearance, putting on a brave face for his next point of call.

It was the war which had brought him to London from his native Wales. At the time when Samuel Jordan had been wooing Alice Lee, Iaan Jones had been on the Somme where, while on a bayonet charge on the German trenches, he had been caught by shrapnel from an exploding shell which had left him with a badly damaged left arm and a scarred face pitted with black metal remnants. Invalided home (and after repairs demobilised as unfit for active service) he had decided against returning to and being something of an oddity in his native village where at least ninety per cent of the men of working age, including his father and two brothers, were coal miners. Unable to do labouring but averse to a job which kept him permanently indoors, he had settled on travelling as an occupation which, in spite of his disability, he could cope with.

Meanwhile, convinced that no woman would marry a man so disfigured, he had accepted bachelor existence philosophically but, deeply regretting having no outlet for his naturally warm and generous nature, had volunteered to help in the local boys' club, only to be rejected on the excuse that his appearance might cause nightmares amongst the more sensitive. Disappointed but accepting this judgement unquestioningly, he had cast around for occupations with which to fill the spare time of a man who society found disturbing and settled on angling as his main hobby.

He bought a bicycle which he kept with Mrs Latta's grudging approval in a shed in the more or less untended garden of number one hundred and three, and thought nothing of cycling thirty miles each way at weekends to a country lake or gravel pit or some secluded pitch on the River Lea or Thames. But his most favourite venue by far was nearer home: the Metropolitan Water Board's reservoirs at Manor Park close by the Brownswood Tennis Club. By dint of applying well in advance, approval to fish these waters was obtainable from the Water Board and whenever a precious permit arrived – usually for a weekday, for the reservoirs were very popular with the local angling cognoscente – Iaan Jones abandoned all thought of selling stationery and took himself off for a blissful day, fishing waters which for all they were scarcely a penny bus ride distant might well have been a hundred miles from London.

Thus he filled his non-working days and appeased the dreams which a casual shell had so cruelly made impossible of fulfilment. Counting his blessings he got on with life – but within him lay an aching need to give of himself to others.

2

"Mr Jones wants to take me fishing, Mummy! He was just

coming out of the lavatory as I came up and he's got an extra permit for tomorrow! Can I go down and tell him that I can?"

Alice looked up from the leg of lamb she was basting to discover Thady, water jug in one hand and the carving knife which he was waving as dangerously as might a charging cavalry man in the other.

"For goodness' sake put that knife down, Thady!" she cried alarmed.

"Yes, Mummy." He had been down with the knife to sharpen it on the whetted Yorkstone entrance steps – a Sunday ritual Tom had taught him.

"*And* that jug before you slop that water everywhere."

"Yes, Mummy. Can I go down and tell him yes. He's waiting!"

"Well, I don't know. You'd better go and ask Pops." 'Pops' was what they'd finally settled on.

"Oh, please, Mummy! Please! If I don't go down right away, he'll probably change his mind and never ask me again."

"Just a minute."

Alice manhandled the joint on its tray into the oven of the mottled-blue gas cooker, checked the gas and closed the door before turning to face Thady. He was smartly turned out for Sunday lunch in shorts and a thin white pullover. Even his socks were for once not around his ankles. She saw the tears of mingled hope and apprehension in his huge, round, blue eyes and the way his full lips trembled. The sight of him wrenched her heart-strings. Every instinct begged her to give approval to his plea. Poor little lamb, he had so few treats, so few toys, so little with which to occupy his days on holiday. He asked so little of her. But there was Tom. It would be risky to go above his head. He'd be upset. She could hear him: 'Micky, we aren't going to get anywhere, you know, if you keep giving the kids approval to do things without consulting me first. I mean, we've been through this times enough; either I'm head of the family or I'm not.' And with his mind occupied with making his lists of books for the twopenny library, they were going through such a good patch.

"Go in and ask Pops," she said.

"He won't say yes. I know he won't say yes!" Thady's voice broke with anguish and the tears began to flow.

She put her arms out towards him. "Come here."

"No."

"Come here." Her voice was very gentle. She took a step towards him and took him in her arms. The smell of his hair was in her nostrils and the wetness from his sobs soaked through her blouse. "Thady," she said. "Listen to me. I want you to go into the bathroom and wash your face and then go upstairs. I'll go down and tell Mr Jones that you've got to ask your father's permission and we'll let him know later what he says. Then I'll go and have a word with Pops and when you hear me go back into the kitchen, then you come down and ask him if you can go with Mr Jones. And try not to cry – you know how it upsets Pops to see you crying."

"I don't like it, Micky."

"But why not, Tom?" Alice asked him from her chair.

He found it difficult. Somewhat similar thoughts were chasing through his mind as had been aired in private by the committee which had considered Iaan Jones' offer to assist them in their boys' club: that far from being convinced of his good intentions, darker motives were suspected – that as it was well known – and had often been discussed by the board – that men whose deformities constrained their opportunity for normal sexual congress were often driven into devious extremities, no risk could be taken that the fellow wouldn't turn out to be a paedophile.

In fact Tom's thoughts did not quite plumb these depths. He did not bring himself to imagining the poor little knocked-about Welshman, as he saw him, actually committing sodomy on

Thady. In fact such a happening was almost beyond his own imagination, but he *could* conceive him fiddling around with Thady's private parts – as he would have put it if he'd had to put it into words. And there was the rub. Because there was simply no way he could explain this to Alice. Such subjects were taboo between men and women. She was, he was fairly certain, quite unaware that such things happened – might even, in spite of the Oscar Wilde business, be unaware that sodomy occurred. Possibly didn't even know the meaning of the word.

So on what grounds did he voice his objections?

"Well, to start with," he said, giving himself time to think, "we're hoping for better things for Thady than spending his spare time fishing with a commercial traveller who hasn't been able to do better for himself than rent a bed-sitter from Mrs Latta."

It's amazing, Alice thought; he really doesn't see himself in the same category as poor Mr Jones, who at least has got a job! And she looked at Tom, seated in the carver chair at the end of the Jacobean-style table – which would soon have to be cleared of his lists and papers for Sunday lunch – smartly enough turned out in a crisp white shirt with an Exiles choker at his neck, and marvelled. It wasn't, as most observers might have thought, casuistry; he really did draw a distinction between men and women who spoke in a certain way and had enjoyed a certain level of education from the rest of mankind in just the same way as he drew a distinction between Englishmen and 'wogs', 'wops' and 'dagoes'. It wouldn't matter how poor they became or how low they sunk, he would still be seeing himself cast in a different mould from those he defined as 'hoi polloi'.

"Well, no, Tom," she agreed. "But just at the moment we're having to be careful until the library starts making money and it is very dull for Dessy and Thady being stuck up here in this lovely weather."

"There's always the park. Or we could buy them a dog. You can get one for five bob. How about that?" It struck him as a brilliant way out.

"Mrs Latta wouldn't agree to it."

"She wouldn't have to know."

"Well, I don't think a dog's a bad idea," Alice said with inspiration. "But we can't get one today and it's tomorrow Mr Jones wants to take Thady fishing. And then if we bought a dog on Tuesday, say, the probability is that he'd be so keen to take it out to Clissold Park or Highbury Fields, he wouldn't want to go fishing with Mr Jones again. Anyway, he mightn't like doing it."

As no new objection had occurred to Tom, this had a certain appeal. After all, if Jones *had* got in mind fiddling around with Thady, he'd probably need a little time before getting round to doing it and by then some better reason for forbidding Thady being alone with him might have surfaced. Anyway, Alice could well be right – Thady mightn't take to fishing and buying a dog had been *his* idea.

He decided to yield but first it was necessary to prepare the ground.

"Well, where's Jones proposing to take him, anyway?"

"He's got permits for one of the reservoirs at Woodberry Down."

"They have fish in them? I thought they were for drinking water."

"No, apparently the fishing's very good. Roach and perch and pike and things like that." And, hastily, "I had a word with Mr Jones who was waiting to hear if Thady could go and I told him it depended on whether or not you approved."

He nodded his head sagely. "Yes," he said thoughtfully and was silent for a while as if turning over important details in his mind.

"I suppose they'd get there by bus," he said. "I know!" It was as if he'd hit on a sovereign solution. "Assuming this weather holds we could go and play some tennis at the Brownswood and, well, maybe Jones could . . . No!" He dismissed the idea. It was too complicated altogether.

"It's a good idea, Tom," Alice said. "But I don't think it would work. Mr Jones would want to go all day. I could fix up Thady with some sandwiches and a bottle of Tizer."

"What about Desmond? I take it he's not included in the invitation?" But, after a moment: "I suppose we could give him sixpence to take himself to the picture palace and buy some sweets. After all, that would be only fair, wouldn't it? Sort of makeweight."

Alice read his mind as if his head was made of glass. He wanted to play tennis and with the boys off their hands there wasn't any reason why they shouldn't.

"You think it's all right then, Tom?"

He nodded. "Just this once, though, Micky. I think it would be a bad thing to make a habit of it."

"I'll call Thady and you can tell him."

"Yes. Do that."

Alice got to her feet. "I'll go and get on with lunch. Perhaps you'll clear the table."

"Yes, of course."

But he had no intention of doing so until after he'd discussed the matter in question with Thady and granted permission – and it was no bad thing for the boy to see that his father was heavily involved.

Thady stood at the opposite end of the table much as he might have stood in front of a schoolmaster's desk. He was not exactly frightened by his stepfather, nor was he awed. If he had to choose a word to describe his feelings towards him he would probably have chosen 'puzzled'. This was the jolly uncle who had hoisted him up on his shoulders that Saturday when he and Desmond had gone shopping with Daddy and Mummy and he had fallen over and grazed his leg; the uncle who had made him super sandcastles on the beach at Shanklin. And he could be a jolly uncle sometimes now. But not too often. More often he could be a cross uncle which he'd never been before, a very cross uncle who shouted and went round slamming doors and making Mummy cry. Except that he wasn't an uncle then. In fact he wasn't really an uncle at all any more – not even when he was jolly. It was difficult to know *what* he was. They'd talked it over, he and Desmond, and Desmond who these days was always reading had said that he was an 'incumbent' now. He hadn't known what that meant and hadn't wanted to admit it to Desmond but he'd looked it up secretly in the Pears Cyclopedia and that had said 'the holder of a benefice' but when he'd looked up 'benefice' the word hadn't been there and he hadn't wanted to ask Desmond to explain because Desmond would have been all superior and talked down to him because he was two years younger. It was funny how everything had changed since they had moved out of Belmont. Uncle Tom had become 'Pops', and wasn't like he had been before; and Desmond wasn't like he had been before when they'd shared a bed and cuddled each other and talked about exchanging heads; and Mummy wasn't like she had been before when she'd been 'Bunty' and had lots and lots of friends and she'd always been going somewhere, smelling nice and in a hurry. She was 'Micky' now and she seemed to be worried all the time that something not very nice was going to happen and she'd suddenly put out her arms and cuddle him or Desmond like she had just now before she'd sent him upstairs and say how much she loved them, that she loved them so much she could squeeze them to death and that 'Pops' loved them too but he'd got a lot on his mind because someone had taken his job away from him but it would be all right and they mustn't ever be worried themselves, he and Desmond, because 'Pops' would get another job or if he didn't then she would but they mustn't ever tell 'Pops' she'd said that to them or he'd get angry. And that was difficult to understand because Mummy had had a job for as long as he could remember and 'Pops' when he'd been Uncle Tom hadn't minded at all.

He looked at his stepfather along the length of the dining table, wondering how to begin, his heart thudding in his chest for fear he'd say it wrongly, and then before he'd had time to work out what to say heard himself blurting out: "Mummy says I'm to ask you if I can go fishing tomorrow with Mr Jones." He knew he should have prefaced it with 'Pops' but for some reason 'Pops' stuck in his throat in a way that 'Uncle Tom' never had. And it was too late now. You couldn't put it on the end of a sentence, could you?

He waited with bated breath.

"Just a minute, Thady," he heard his stepfather say. "There's one or two things I've got to finish first. Just sit down. I won't be long."

So he sat in the other carver and watched while Tom ran a pencil down a list he had in front of him, paused with the pencil point pressed on something on the list, then nodded approvingly and wrote something with the pencil in a notebook he had beside him. He did this two or three times before he put the pencil down and leaned back in his chair with both hands on the table edge.

"Yes, Thady?" he said as if he hadn't heard and didn't know why Thady was there at all.

"Mummy says . . ." He broke off and began again: "Pops, Mummy says I'm to ask you if it's all right to go fishing with Mr Jones. Tomorrow. At the reserve—" He fumbled the word.

"Reservoir," Pops said helpfully.

Thady nodded eagerly. "Mummy told you?"

"Yes, Thady, she did."

"And is it all right?"

"Well, yes. This once."

Thady's mouth dropped open. Mr Jones had said if he enjoyed it, he could go again when Mr Jones got another permit. Or maybe go up to Hampstead Heath and fish for pike in the pond below Jack Straw's Castle which sounded exciting.

"You mean I can't go again if Mr Jones asks me to?"

"I think it would be better if you didn't."

"Why?"

"You have to understand, Thady," Tom said sententiously, having used the interval as he thought wisely, "that people of different backgrounds don't really fit well together. There's an old saying: oil and water don't mix. That's a very good saying you should always remember. Mr Jones' family, his brothers and his father are coal miners."

"So was Mummy's grandad."

"Don't be cheeky!" Tom, who had made an effort over many months to put this unpalatable fact out of his mind, retorted angrily.

"I wasn't being cheeky."

"You're being cheeky now."

Thady noticed that his stepfather's cheeks were, of a sudden, pink – which he'd learnt was a sign which often preceded raised voices and doors being slammed. He resisted pointing out that if to deny an accusation was to be accused of it, it was impossible to have a conversation.

So he sat in silence feeling lost in the vastness of the second carver wondering what to do with his arms and whether resting them on the arms of the carver like Pops' were would be considered cheeky too. And Tom, reasonably satisfied with Thady's silence, stared at him gravely, noting with distaste that the boy had been crying recently and looked as if at any minute he might start again and, observing the fullness of his lips, thinking that what he needed was a year or two at a school where the discipline was strict enough to toughen him up and tighten them.

"And it's not only a question of the oil and water business, Thady," he said considerately. "There are some men who behave in funny ways." He held up a warning finger. "I'm not saying Mr Jones does, you understand. Mr Jones is a very brave man who's suffered badly because of the war." He wondered why he'd put that in – it wasn't just irrelevant but it had thrown him off track. And also it might lead the boy to ask why he hadn't served in the war which wouldn't have been that easy to explain. "But we don't know him very well and until one knows a man well one can't be sure that he won't do things to little boys that he oughtn't to." And, quickly, "And I'm not going to explain that because it isn't something that's pleasant to talk about and the probability is that you wouldn't understand me anyway. But I'll just say this: that if Mr Jones suggests you stop fishing and go somewhere else with him, you're not to go. Do you understand?"

Thady nodded dumbly.

"And if he starts . . . well, doing things that aren't . . . that you don't think are right for him to do to you, you've got to tell him not to and that you're going to tell your father about it as soon as you get home."

"Yes, Pops," Thady said – but without the least intention of complying, for yet another criticism of his stepfather had been added to his list.

There had been a sequel to the Morris Sams episode at St Olive's. In defending himself Sams had laid the blame on Mr Forbury – who taught English, History and Scripture and had been at the school since Colonel Latham's days – accusing him of seducing him into buggery in the first place. In some relief when she heard this accusation, Mrs Latham, who had been seeking an excuse to replace Mr Forbury anyway, had summoned a sort of Star Chamber which only Doctor Donleavy, Mr Forbury and herself attended. Mr Forbury, a mild, untidy little man rejected Sams' accusation out of hand and Mrs Latham generously agreed to give him the benefit of the doubt and look no further into the matter subject to his giving immediate notice. By the next day Forbury had gone and

Doctor Donleavy, flanked by Mrs Latham and Captain Elliott, addressed the school *en masse*, informed them of Mr Forbury's departure and without actually making any connection between the two told them that Sams had been led astray, was repentant, had sworn on the Bible never to offend in the way he had again and was being given a second but final chance. And before dismissing them to their classrooms Doctor Donleavy delivered a stirring message:

"Boys of St Olive's! Wicked forces have been at work and some of you have suffered grievously at the hands of one of your number who has been corrupted by an older man. Appropriate punishment has been meted out to those who have offended and solemn undertakings have been received that there will never again be any repetition. Now the time has come to put the past behind us and turn our thoughts to the future which lies ahead for all of us. To dwell on what has happened would be a valueless exercise and the sooner we blot from our minds the evil that has occurred, the sooner will the sore which has afflicted this fine school be healed. I adjure you all here and now to enter into a solemn commitment and join with me, Mrs Latham and all the other members of the staff never to disclose to any living person one word of what has happened. To do so would reflect not only on the honour of the school itself and those of us who have your interests so deeply at heart, but on yourselves."

The sting in the tail of this peroration was subsequently underlined by individual chats with each of the little boys known to have been buggered by Sams to the effect that telling their parents what had happened would only cause them unhappiness and that although it was not their fault the world at large would think the less of them if it discovered they had, however involuntarily, taken part in a vile and illegal exercise.

The upshot of all this and the endless discussions between the pupils of St Olive's which had naturally followed was that Thady understood perfectly well what his stepfather was getting at and marvelled that he could be so ignorant about what boys of his age knew. There had been moments when he had been tempted to break the vow of silence extorted from him by Doctor Donleavy but the pusillanimous dissembling of his stepfather who, while not daring to face the issue, sought (as Thady saw it) to extract profit from it, convinced him that it would be as good as useless at any time to seek advice from him on any matters of importance and if ever the time came when he felt like disclosing secrets of his heart, this was the last man on earth that he should go to.

Eleven

1929

1

Grahame Culverwell let himself into his Highgate house, hung his hat on the hallstand, went through into the sitting room which faced a large walled garden, said, "Hallo, Bee," to his wife (who, relaxed on a *chaise-longue* and head down in a playscript, raised a perfectly manicured acknowledging hand), crossed to the cocktail cabinet, poured two Fino Innocentes and put one on her side table before relaxing into his armchair.

"You know who called in on me today, Bee?" he called to her. "Alice Jordan. Who's now Alice Fenwick!"

Beatrice Culverwell put in a bookmarker and, closing the playscript she had been considering, laid it down beside her sherry. She was a tall, slim American woman of surpassing elegance who dressed with the intelligence and taste becoming to the wife of a man who made beautiful clothes. For the autumn evening she was dressed in a Chanel jersey suit with a busy top and a small check side-pleated skirt cut just below the knee. As a matter of principle she never wore anything which came from her husband's collections.

"That her new trade name?" she suggested.

He shook his head. "New husband."

Beatrice thought for a few moments, drawing a mental image of the eager young woman who had bluffed her way into becoming her husband's dress designer, proved herself and then persuaded him to finance her in her own gown venture.

"I'm surprised she's married again," she said. "I know I only met her a couple of times but I always saw her as quite dedicated to a career." She took a cork-tipped cigarette from a silver cigarette box and fitted it into a long amber holder but paused before lighting it, shaking her head and making her long metal earrings sway. "No, of course," she said. "She sold her business, didn't she? You helped advise her how best to do it." She lit the cigarette and exhaled a long thin column of smoke. "The first one was something of an intellectual, wasn't he? What does the new one do?"

"He doesn't do anything at the moment. Apparently he was in wireless telegraphy but lost his job when the company he worked for got taken over last year and hasn't done anything since except get involved in one these twopenny library things that hasn't worked out."

A wry smile touched her carefully painted lips. "She waits for Wall Street to crash before she calls on you. Hardly the best of timing!" She transferred her cigarette-holder to the other hand and held it a long way away from her. Like the long, dangling earrings, the exaggerated holder suited her but in fact she didn't use it for effect but because she hated smoke getting in her eyes. "What does she want from you? Her old job back?"

"Financial backing."

"You going to give it her?"

"No."

"Why not? Worked out all right last time, didn't it?"

He nodded. "Yes. But what she's got in mind isn't in my bailiwick."

"So what has she got in mind?"

"Cheap dresses produced in quantity under her own brand name. She's even thought of one. Holly Wood Dresses!"

"Hollywood!" She sounded as if she had never heard anything more unbelievable in her life.

He chuckled. "No. Two words. Holly Wood! It was Paquette after Paquin; now it's to be Holly Wood after Hollywood."

"Well, I think it's dreadful. Holly Wood Dresses! What's it supposed to mean? Dresses imported from the States? Or designed by a woman named Holly Wood? Why not Alice Jordan Dresses? Or Gowns? Or better still – Alice Gowns! That's got punch!"

"You've got a point," he agreed.

He crossed the room, which was large and well proportioned with three tall windows overlooking the garden, to refill his glass. Over a fine Adams chimney piece in which a newly-lit fire burned comfortingly – for it was a cold October day – was a Maurice Utrillo of a street scene which, with its muted colours, fallen leaves and bare autumn trees, could in the proper season almost have been painted outside the house. In one corner there was a Steinway grand piano whose lack of ornaments suggested it was regularly played upon; there was a tall, filled bookcase and as well as the *chaise-longue* and two or three armchairs, a settee facing a long, narrow marble-topped table. The floor was of a deep, rich wood scattered with cheerful and interesting rugs, the window drapes had a Regency motif and were professionally done with deep moulded pelmets. There were two fine chandeliers. A gramophone with a massive horn and a rather shiny cocktail cabinet made the point that the Culverwells weren't slaves to tradition and in fact the whole room projected an atmosphere of being fully lived in and enjoyed by its owners.

Beatrice watched him as he refilled his glass, Although the news he had brought home with him interested her, she was in no hurry to ask her questions. They shared a good understanding, yet lived their own separate lives. She knew enough about his business to be both companion and sounding-board and he, although scrupulously taking no part in them, was genuinely fascinated by her theatrical activities.

She waited until he was back in his chair before saying:

"Anyway, forgetting the name, you haven't said why you aren't going to help her, Gra'ame." She always pronounced his name without the aspirate.

"Because it isn't my range. I'm couture – this is inexpensive ready-made garments for the masses. I'm not investing money in something I don't understand."

She pulled at the mass of beads hung around her neck – a habit she kept vainly trying to cure.

"That figures," she agreed. "How much is she looking for?"

"A thousand."

"Is that all?"

"All she's looking for. For it to work she'd need a good deal more."

"Has she any money of her own?"

"Apparently not."

"You've got to hand it to her. The girl's got guts."

Grahame Culverwell chuckled. "That's a quality she's never been lacking in."

"But you aren't going to help her this time?"

"No."

"Well, you are."

He looked at her, surprised. She was back to relaxing in her *chaise-longue*, cigarette-holder between her lips supported by two fingers on one of which was a ring of little value but almost obscene size. An American woman who preferred the English way of life; an entrepreneur hard-bitten in her chosen career as West End impresario yet kind and very human outside of it.

"What am I going to do, Bee?" he said.

"You're going to invite her, without this new husband she's got, to come and have dinner with us here and I'm going to invite Solly."

"Solly!" He was astonished. It was difficult to imagine two more dissimilar human beings than Alice Fenwick and Solly Kornblath. And why should Kornblath – who was Beatrice's principal theatrical angel – be interested in backing something so totally outside his line?

"But he knows nothing about the fashion business," he objected.

"He knew nothing about theatre when he started putting money into it."

"You're telling me you think you can persuade Solly Kornblath, over a dinner table, to put money into the rag trade! I don't believe it, Bee."

"You're probably right. But it would be fun to have a try. And I'm not going to be the one doing the persuading. That'll be up to her."

2

The failure of the twopenny library project had forced a move into a semi-basement flat whose rent was, usefully, less than Mrs Latta's for the maisonette and, with little now with which to occupy his time, Tom Fenwick had taken to lying in bed until quite late on in the morning so that Alice, who received few letters, was able to intercept Culverwell's which was very much to the point.

Bolton House
Pond Square
Highgate N19
Telephone Number: Highgate 731

October 23rd, 1929

Dear Alice,
Will you give me a ring at the office. I have a thought which might just be helpful in getting this crackpot idea of yours off the ground.
Yours sincerely,
Grahame

Alice stood stock still by the doorway to the dark passage leading to the flat.

"What is it, Micky?" she heard Tom calling from the bedroom.

"Nothing," she lied. "Nothing. Just a circular."

She hurried along the passage as excited and guilty as a married woman with a letter from her lover fearful of being caught out by her husband. She went through the bathroom into the lavatory and, bolting the door behind her, tore the envelope into shreds and flushed the pieces down the pan. The paper was of a thick parchment type in that several pieces resisted dispatch and, while she waited for the cistern to fill, by the light of the tiny window glazed with obscured glass which prevented them having even as much of a glimpse of their landlord's garden, she re-read the letter. But she had scarcely done so before she heard Tom's heavy tread into the bathroom and, having looked wildly round her vainly seeking a hiding place for the letter itself, thrust it inside her blouse.

There was a rattling on the door as Tom tried it.

"I'm in here, Tom," she called.

"Oh, sorry."

She listened to his retreating footsteps, then pulled the chain. The cistern hadn't quite filled but flushed sufficiently to get rid of all but two of the offending bits of envelope, one face up, the ink already running. She picked them out and with inspired imagination stood on the pan seat and poked them into the cistern through the hole where the lever worked. Then to give verisimilitude to her actions she waited for a few more seconds before quitting the lavatory.

She found Tom in the kitchen, dressed in pyjamas with slippers on his feet. He was gaining weight steadily now and there was a puffiness to his face which had smudged away what once had been reasonable looks. He was by the chipped stone sink, pouring himself a glass of water. Behind the sink there was a sash window which, like its fellow in the lavatory, had been glazed with opaque glass making it impossible to look into the extensive garden which lay mysterious and never seen behind. Through the glass could be seen iron burglar bars; the window itself was quite immovable, either jammed shut through warping or perhaps screwed shut from the outer side.

The flat was, remarkably, in Aberdeen Park and not far removed from Cranmore Hotel to which Alice had retreated while securing her divorce. It had two bedrooms and a sitting room, all semi-basement, and the kitchen had once been a coal cellar, the coal being poured in from a coal hole in front of the generous flight of steps which gave access to the massive Edwardian, Italianate house above in which their landlord lived. The back portion of the kitchen was still a coal cellar but the front walls had been whitewashed and a gas stove installed. The kitchen teemed with mice which resisted all efforts at extermination and which, while in daytime largely keeping to this area, could be found from time to time anywhere in the flat.

Such were the quarters to which Alice and her boys had been reduced. It had been an awful year and more. It had taken a full six months before Tom had even bestirred himself to seek employment and, pitching his valuation of his own abilities too high, had utterly failed to find it. To Alice's chagrin this had apparently not particularly disturbed him. He had comforted himself with the absurd persuasion that the twopenny library would in the end yield dividends and by the time it failed so badly that even Sachs – who Joseph had correctly prophesied would only step in to pick up the pieces cheaply if worthwhile – had not bothered to do anything, he had become curiously habituated to leading the life of a man of leisure.

Eking out some sort of existence on his pension of two pounds a week, the remnants of his compensation money and the little remaining in Alice's Post Office account, they had survived but to do so had been forced to move to this dingy semi-basement flat. Continued membership of the Brownswood Club had been beyond their means but occasionally Tom managed a game of tennis by sharing a sixpenny fee with one of its members to hire for an hour a public court in Highbury Fields. Meanwhile, Desmond and Thady, with any form of private school not to be thought of, and public school thereafter not to be imagined, had been taken away from St Olive's and were attending respectively Highbury County School where the fee was twelve pounds a year and Drayton Park Council School which was free.

The obvious solution was for Alice to get a job herself but with Tom obstinately setting his face against it, declaring manfully, 'No wife of mine goes out to work. When I asked you to marry me, I gave you my word it wasn't anything you would ever have to do again and my word's my bond!', she was on the horns of a dilemma.

He was as much in love with her as he had ever been and, within the frustrating limits of the way of life he had dragged her down to, was most of the time a pleasant enough companion. Buoyed up by an extraordinary optimism that if, as he refused to believe, the twopenny library folded, he would easily find a way of filling the gap in their finances and with, for a time, an unlimited supply of books at his disposal, he settled into a life of total indolence, 'keeping out of the way', as he put it, while Alice got up and made breakfast for Desmond and Thady before packing them off to walk to school, rising in mid-morning to settle with a book in an armchair if it was raining or perhaps taking himself off for a swim in the free baths at the end of Highbury Fields if it was fine. And so on through the day. There were times when Alice could have screamed aloud as she watched him spend twenty minutes polishing and buffing up his brogues or a full two hours devouring a newspaper, column inch by column inch, while she cooked and sewed and turned up hems and unpicked materials to make them up again.

Only once since being here had her control snapped and she had accused him of rank laziness, thrown his promises in his face, reproached him for his stupidity in wasting his compensation money and taunted him for his uselessness. And the result had been exactly as it had been before. Slamming doors so hard they made the whole flat shiver, he had taken himself off and a week's drinking bout had followed.

But for the children she would have have faced reality earlier than she did. In the Highbury New Park maisonette, when drink turned the Jeykll she had married into a Hyde, at least they had been able to seek safety in the upper floor; but here, where they had to share a double bed because there was room for nothing more in a room only yards away from where mayhem was going on, there was no way of escaping from his yelling and rampaging and she imagined them huddled and trembling in each others' arms, awaiting the moment their door was flung open and he came in to murder them. I have to protect them, there is no one else, she told herself. It's me who brought this on them. If I have to endure this hand-to-mouth existence, this sense that nothing can ever change, that ahead of us stretch endless years in which we go nowhere and do nothing stimulating, in which life has become not just a dull routine but a tightrope existence in which I have to control my temper and treat my husband as if he were fine china for fear that otherwise I will spark off another outburst, then so be it.

The Wall Street crash, the effects of which reverberated around the world ruining millions, came as a lifeline. The twopenny library was one of its earliest casualties. Twopence bought a good deal – a couple of herrings for supper, a packet of Woodbine cigarettes, two pounds of potatoes, a large loaf of bread or a quart of milk – and the bank manager (who had been barely persuaded to back the venture anyway), concluding that most people would rather use money for such essentials than for the brief use of a book, called in the loan. There were insufficient funds to meet it but, fortunately, unlike Samuel Jordan who had regarded companies as immoral institutions, Alan Sachs had believed in them as enthusiastically as did Joseph Mott and while all subscribed capital was lost, in this case at least Alice was able to keep clothes, jewellery and furniture.

Even before the Wall Street crash not only were the country's finances in a disastrous state anyway, but from all manner of directions it seemed beset by new and unimagined problems. There were threats from every quarter whether it be from de Valera in Ireland or from Mahatma Gandhi in India. The newspapers were filled with doleful verdicts on the present and gloomy prognostications for the future. Unemployment was soaring; strikes, demonstrations and hunger marches were becoming the order of the day. And, to cap it all, the unimaginable had happened: a second Labour government under Ramsay Macdonald had been returned to power.

Alice, aware by now that the man she had married lived by the stock notions and habits drilled into him by a harsh despot of a father, concluded that, could she but use it properly, here was an instrument she could turn to good account. She saw that all the old values and criteria by which he had run his life would seem to him to be in the balance. If, she reasoned, at this time when we are under so much pressure, I can give him a sufficient excuse, surely I can persuade him to abandon this obstinate refusal to allow me to go and do something about it. It isn't only he's stuffed to the hilt with the prejudice that his wife shouldn't work, perhaps what's equally important is that he sees in the idea of his wife working his own abilities shown to the world as lacking. But if through the ineptness of others and the malign influence of a disaster occurring thousands of miles away he can be made to feel that the platform from which he *could* succeed has been swept away from under him, then won't he have an ironclad excuse for being like the millions of others like him who simply cannot find a job? Surely it must be so. Surely he'll have the sense not to go off the deep end and rush out to the pub if I'm able to offer a positive solution.

And there, she saw, was the rub. To talk vaguely, even optimistically, about being able to go out and earn money wouldn't do; she had to present him with something so assured that the alternative between the way of life they were leading now and the way of life they could be leading if, to use his own over-used expression, he 'fell into line' was stark and clear. And more than that, whatever it was she did offer him had to be dressed up in such a way that it would be acceptable.

For weeks she had mulled this over with the greater problem not seeming to be the actual gaining of employment but that of summoning up enough courage to run the risk that her reasoning was sound. Having decided the risk must be taken she had secretly (only by the most devious excuses somehow finding the time to do so) followed up such few advertisements as there were for dress designers and drawn a total blank. The realisation that things were even more difficult than she had supposed merely hardened her resolve. She must, she saw, think of some new angle, have something to offer a prospective employer that he had not had offered to him before.

It was while poring through a fashion magazine she found the inspiration she was needing. It came in one word: *sizing*. The magazine had an agony column to which readers wrote with their dressmaking problems and in one of these Alice read a complaint that buying even ready-made dresses was quite beyond the writer's means – because of her particular size they never fitted and she had invariably to take them somewhere to have expensive alterations made.

But how absurd, thought Alice. The woman's absolutely right of course – it was happening all the time to my dresses at Paquette. Like everyone else, I only made three or four normal sizes and none of them catered for the larger figure. And with things as they are, with every penny counting, the outsize woman, or perhaps the very small woman, who might just be persuaded to go and buy a new dress is going to be put off by knowing it's going to cost her half as much again to have it altered before it's fit for her to wear! But suppose there was a firm, with its own brand name, who made such a range of sizes that almost every woman could buy off the peg and be satisfied? And suppose that firm swamped the magazines with its advertisements? Advertisements which cashed in on the very slump we're going through, the slump that looks like going on and on for years, by extolling the savings which could be made. Surely it must succeed? Why *hasn't* anyone thought of this before?

She could hardly restrain herself. Like anyone who has what is believed to be an original brainwave, she lay awake at night, tossing and turning in the fear that someone else would think of it before she could put it into production. And it was no good, she reasoned, offering it as an idea. It would simply be stolen from her. No, she must work it out, put it together, smooth the edges, and offer it as a package to someone she could trust. And running through her mind all the people she had met and known through her Paquette years, she dismissed them all. All but one – Grahame Culverwell. And so she had called in on him and he had been kind and patient but, so she had assumed, dismissed the idea out of hand.

But now there was this letter – the one which was burning a hole inside her blouse. The letter Tom mustn't know she had received.

He looked at her, glass of water in his hand: stocky, somewhat overweight, unshaven, clad in pyjamas, still with clear blue eyes and thick wavy hair but no longer the young man who had turned hearts in Belmont.

"What was it? The circular?" he said.

"Well, I don't really know. I tore it up and flushed it down the lavatory." What else could she say – he must know she hadn't had time to get rid of it elsewhere.

"What an extraordinary thing to do."

She realised from the glint in his eyes that he didn't believe her.

"Well, we get so many of the damn things," she said. "Are you ready for breakfast or would you rather get dressed first?" She moved as if to start making preparations and as she passed near enough for him to do so, he reached out a hand and grasped her arm. The grip was like a band of steel. He was still so strong that he could sit with his elbow on a table, his lower arm raised and the combined efforts of Desmond and Thady couldn't pull it down.

"You're lying to me, Micky, aren't you?" he said.

"No."

"Yes, you are. You've had a letter from someone, haven't you? A letter you don't want me to see."

"No, Tom. I promise you. It was just a circular."

"I never thought the day would come when you'd lie to me."

The glint in his eyes had turned to anger. My God, he probably thinks I've got a lover! she thought.

"You've still got the letter, haven't you?" he said. "Where is it? Inside your blouse or hidden in the bathroom or the lavatory?"

The blouse was made of white crêpe de Chine and it wasn't at all impossible he could see the shape of the letter through the material. In the unpredictable state anger drove him into, he might take it into his head to rip it open. She had to make an immediate decision.

"All right, Tom," she admitted. "I have lied to you. Please let go of my arm and I'll explain."

But if anything his grip tightened. "It's from a man, isn't it?" he accused her.

"As a matter of fact it is. But it isn't what you think."

"I want that letter!" he exploded. "You hear me, woman! The letter!"

There was no question of it. He believed it *was* from a lover and was consumed with jealousy.

"You're hurting me," she said.

"Hurting you! Jesus Christ, I'll do more than that if it's what I think it is. I'll kill you!" In his rage his voice rang out so loudly she wondered if their landlords, the Stringers, who lived in the house above them, could hear him. She half expected to hear the hammering on the floor which had sometimes accompanied his outbursts through that ghastly week of his drinking bout.

"It's from Culverwell," she said. "It's about my going out to work."

There. It was said. Out of the right time, out of the wrong context, it was said.

And it was as if she had struck him in the face. His hand fell off her arm, he physically recoiled. Swiftly, seizing this moment while he was off balance, she reached inside her blouse, took out the letter and handed it to him. "There!" she said. "Read it yourself! And don't ever again accuse me of being untrue to you."

He took the letter with a hand that shook, read it, scrunched it to a ball and hurled it purposelessly at the wall.

"You've been deceiving me, woman, haven't you!" he said. "You've been behind my back seeing this pansy Culverwell."

"Pansy?" she said, amazed. "What are you talking about?"

"He has to be a pansy. No man worth his salt would make a living in the rag trade!"

She realised he was back to his old mental gymnastics, reaching blindly for anything to cover up his bungling, hauling in a prejudice for lack of anything constructive and thought out to say.

"He's a kind and decent married man," she told him. "For whom I worked as you know full well for a very long time. He isn't a pansy and even if he was it wouldn't matter. In fact I would have thought you'd have been pleased as a moment or two ago you were suspecting me of having an affair with him."

"I was not."

"Yes, you were," she said, holding her ground. "I went to see him because I have an idea which can get us out of this mess we wouldn't have been in if you'd done what you said you were going to do and used your money to set me" – she corrected herself hastily – "to set us up in business instead of wasting half of it in that stupid lending library nonsense and frittering the other half away in the Highbury Barn!"

"If it hadn't been for this bloody American business, it would have worked out fine."

She seized on that. She saw that he was totally confused. Torn by emotion, guilty at his false assessment of the situation, embarrassed at having his own uselessness thrown in his face, unsure how to extricate himself with any semblance of dignity.

"Look at it!" she stormed, throwing out her bruised, sore arm. "We live in a pigsty that crawls with mice. We have two boys of nine and eleven who have to sleep in the same double bed at their ages because we haven't the money to buy single beds for them and even if we had there wouldn't be room to put them in. We send them to council schools where they have to mix with the children of dustmen – and road sweepers – and . . . and . . ." She had run out of ideas. "Of sandwichboard men!" she managed. "And what do *you* do about it? You who are always talking about the importance of having a public school education. Even though you didn't have one yourself!"

There, that was out too. Except that Dessy and Thady were at school instead of in the Slit, it was horribly like that morning in Stradbroke Road when she'd torn her first marriage to shreds. And just like then, she didn't care.

"What do you do about it?" she raged. "Nothing! You lie in bed waited on hand and foot as if . . . as if you were a member of the landed gentry you're so proud we have. Well, I'm not. I'm working-class. I wasn't brought up to believe that so long as you were entitled to wear a blazer with a badge on it the world owed you a living as you seem to think it does! I was brought up to believe that if you wanted to have anything, you had to go out to work to get it. And that's what I'm going to do! And you're not going to stop me. You can go out to the pub and come back sottishly drunk and start knocking me about, but it's not going to make any difference. I'm going to go out and make money. Lots of money. I'm going to get out of this slum you've condemned me to living in by your own idleness and prejudice and stupidity. And if you behave yourself then maybe you can come with me and maybe not!" Her eyes lighted on the ball of the letter on the scratched linoleum floor. She strode past him, pushing him aside because he was partly in her way and in doing so felt the softness of his swelling belly. "You're getting fat," she taunted him. "And no wonder. Lying around like you do all day. You go on with the life you're living much longer and you won't even be able to play a decent game of tennis." She paused. "And then what'll you do? When you've become useless at games as well? At the only thing you've ever been good at in your life. And your wife's out at work all day and all you've got to buy popularity in some stinking pub with is your miserable two pounds a week pension money!" She picked up the scrunched-up letter and started to straighten it out, wondering at his unwillingness or inability to respond. "Well?" she charged him. "Haven't you got anything to say?"

But he stood silent, baffled. She hated what she had done and was at the same time relieved, even proud that she had done it.

"You'd better get your own breakfast," she said. "I'm going out to telephone Grahame Culverwell and I don't know when I'm going to be back. In fact you'd better get your own lunch as well. Whatever happens I won't be back until it's time to get Dessy and Thady their tea."

She left him, standing there, a forlorn and defeated man in striped pyjamas, still unshaven at ten in the morning.

3

After she had gone, Tom's immediate instinct was to pull on some clothes and make for the Highbury Barn and he was only persuaded against doing so by the realisation that there was a full two hours before the pubs would open. And so instead, having slammed a few doors to ease his anger, he sat himself down at the kitchen table and with his chin in his cupped hands pondered on Alice's diatribe.

They had had rows enough before, but never had she launched on him such bitter and violent criticism and the more his anger cooled the more he admitted to himself the justification of almost everything that she had said and the more he quailed at the picture she had painted of what lay ahead for him. All through his life he had striven to hide his weaknesses not just from the world but from himself and to a degree, through his prowess at games, his popularity amongst men and women who knew him only casually and by loyally clinging to the stock notions and habits his overbearing father had drummed into him, he had succeeded. But nothing now was left to him. Like a woman tearing from a pad a sheet of paper on which his character, his hopes, his very future had been written and scrunching it to a ball to fling it contemptuously into a wastepaper basket, Alice had stripped away such veneer as still remained and exposed his naked soul.

"And it is rotten!" The words, spoken aloud, were his own.

For a full hour, perhaps even longer, he sat at the table, mulling over all that Alice had said, going through it in extraordinary detail, accusation followed by accusation, taunt by taunt, threat by threat, prophecy by prophecy – and the whole of it, seen together, terrifying in its awfulness and accuracy, showed him to be a ranting, raging, vaunting, boasting, blustering, swaggering man of straw, useless to himself, an encumbrance to all who found themselves obliged to live with him.

There was, he saw, only one solution; only one thing he could do, if not to make amends then at least to free the woman he loved so desperately and to give her children a better chance of a decent upbringing than they could ever hope for in his company.

Sitting at the kitchen table he wrote a note and when it was finished, re-read it, nodded approvingly, signed it, put it in an envelope which he addressed to her and left it on the kitchen table and then, with a change of mind, took it into the sitting room and put it on the Jacobean table. The mice, he reflected wryly, wouldn't be able to get at it there – the only things in the flat which seemed to defeat them were the ornate pillars which supported it.

There was, he told himself, no hurry and a man going to his death should prepare himself properly for it. So he went into the bathroom and, while the geyser boomed and roared filling the bath, shaved carefully. Then lying in the water he pondered on the appropriate way to kill himself and, having decided, chuckled at his decision, dressed in his plus-fours outfit, put on his brogues and quit the flat.

There was no need to go to Lillywhites, he told himself; there was that firm in Holloway Road, who as they made billiard tables presumably stocked snooker balls and very likely had some old ones going cheaply. It wasn't far to walk – there was no point in wasting money going by bus. In any case he'd have to change at Highbury Corner. So he walked up the gravelled pavement of Aberdeen Park and, crossing Highbury Grove, made his way across Highbury Fields and down Ronalds Road. He crossed Holloway Road continuing along to the store where, as he had correctly hoped, he was able to buy a second-hand set of snooker balls which, as it happened, were missing the green and brown, but that didn't matter.

With the balls in a carrier bag he walked up to Highbury Corner and caught a bus to Hyde Park Corner and from there a Green Line bus to Maidenhead. Disembarking at the stop nearest the bridge he made his way to the firm from which he had always hired punts before and, insisting they provided him with an anchor, hired another one and punted his way through and upstream of Boulter's Lock. When he was, as best as he could remember, opposite the place where he had made love to Alice, he shipped the punt pole and dropped the anchor. Then, taking a good look around him to make certain he was not observed, he undid the belt of his plus fours and distributed the snooker balls equally down into the legs. Having done so, he did up his belt, pulled on the anchor to make sure it held fast enough and there was no danger of the punt breaking loose and being carried away to its destruction on the weir, manoeuvred himself to sit on the side of it and slipped overboard.

4

There are few of us who cannot trace at least one, and usually more than one occasion, when the course of our life has been drastically re-directed by some trivial happening. We pause to raise an umbrella and, because of the few seconds' delay this causes, meet on a traffic island a friend we have not seen since our schooldays and through whom we will maybe go on to meet the man or the woman we will marry or perhaps be introduced to people through whose association our future business affairs will be crowned with success or brought low by disaster.

And the converse equally applies for there have to be innumerable occasions when, unknown to us, through failing to take some minor action, our lives carry on in an unchanging course when they could so easily have been diverted into other channels.

So it was with Alice on this disappointing late October morning which was utterly to change her own life, her children's lives and the lives of countless other human beings.

Mr Culverwell was out. She had missed him by just ten minutes. His reasons for being out, if not as trivial as pausing to raise an umbrella, were of small moment – he had just left to have a fitting for a suit and afterwards to have his hair cut. "No, Mrs Fenwick," she was told by the loquacious Miss Giffey who managed the tiny switchboard, "I shouldn't think he'll be back for a couple of hours. Why don't you try him again about twelve thirty. He's almost certain to be in before going out to lunch." And she went on to enquire at considerable length as to how Alice was, and how her children were and what she was doing now and to comment on such matters as the weather and Mr Gandhi's curious mode of dress on his recent visit to England.

Escaping at last, Alice quit the telephone kiosk and stood on the glistening, drizzled pavement of Highbury Grove, frustrated and uncertain and to a degree deflated. Two hours; what on earth could she do to fill in two hours? She couldn't go back to the flat; not immediately after giving Tom that piece of her mind. You couldn't march out in such fine fettle buoyed up with resolve and purpose only to return five minutes later no further forward than when you'd left!

So what should she do? How fill in the next two hours? If she had a local friend, an intimate, she could call in on, that would be an answer. But she had no friends, no real friends, only acquaintances, people she'd known in Belmont, or with Tom at the Brownswood Tennis Club. And for one reason or another she was cut adrift from even those groups now.

If it had been a pleasant autumn morning she might have sat for a while on a bench in Highbury Fields just across the road from Highbury Grove – and had she chosen to do so, she could not have missed seeing Tom on his way to buy his snooker balls and with her passion calmed by the sheer passage of time as like as not the tragedy of his suicide would have been averted. But although the drizzle had ceased it was a dull sort of morning and far too cool for just sitting around.

There was shopping she had to do but there was the possibility that Culverwell would want to see her to explain this 'thought' which obviously could be of vital importance to her or he wouldn't have told her he had it, and while it wasn't likely he *would* want to see her it was not impossible and she could hardly turn up with a couple of carrier bags filled with groceries and vegetables.

So in the end, bereft of more positive ideas, Alice walked to Highbury Barn and bought a fashion magazine, and then – on the basis that if Culverwell did want to see her urgently and might have little time to spare, it would be better if she was that much nearer to him – caught a bus to the Angel and killed an hour over the magazine and a pot of tea in Lyons Corner House before telephoning him again.

This time she was lucky – he was in. With a heart beating absurdly fast, she waited while Miss Giffey, after her usual irrelevancies, put her through.

"Alice. You've had my letter then?"

"Yes, Mr Culverwell."

"Well, look. There may not be anything in this so I don't want to build the possibilities too high, but my wife has had an idea which she thinks just might work."

"Yes, Mr Culverwell?"

"There's a man she knows whose name is Kornblath, Solomon Kornblath. He's Jewish of course and inconceivably rich. He backs some of Beatrice's plays and he's a bit of a gambler anyway. Well, she wondered, just wondered, Alice, if it was possible to persuade him to back your Holly Wood Dresses idea. And she phoned him and he seemed to be interested—"

"But that's marvellous!"

"Just a minute, just a minute! Do let me finish." It was said with a good-natured chuckle.

"I'm sorry."

"He seemed to be interested in meeting you to talk about it. Beatrice had in mind inviting the two of you to have dinner with us at Highgate but Kornblath told her that if he was going to see you it would have to be you by yourself and at his offices in Berkeley Square and that you had to be the one to fix a time and date. All right?"

"Well, yes, of course, but . . ." She broke off. It was bewildering.

"Now, don't worry, Alice," Culverwell said reassuringly. "And don't pitch your hopes too high. And whatever you do, don't try and get in touch with Kornblath until you've spoken to Beatrice first. She knows the man inside out and there's probably no one better to advise you what to tell him and what not to tell him."

"I'll telephone her right away. If you can let me know her number . . ."

In his office, the telephone held to his ear, Grahame Culverwell was smiling at her eagerness and remembering very clearly the day she had cast before him the dreadful sketches which represented her clumsy efforts at stealing bits and pieces of other people's designs and putting them together as inspirations of her own, clumsy sketches which proved she had never so much as designed a dress in her life but possessed an innate and astonishing instinct as to what would sell. He knew that Beatrice didn't really hold out much more hope for Alice than perhaps a modest contribution from her wealthy friend – but then, as he told himself, he hadn't held out much hope for her when first they'd met. And against all the odds, she'd persuaded him. Who knows, he thought, she might even work a miracle with Solly Kornblath!

"No, don't do that," he advised her. "If you phone her at

the office you might catch her in the middle of a meeting and she won't be able to give you her full attention. Phone her at home this evening. You've got the number, it's on my letter. Highgate 731."

"Yes," said Alice, for want of anything better to say. "I've got the number." And she had. The letter, straightened from its crumpling, was in her handbag.

"About seven would be a good time, Alice. And . . ." with a pause, "good luck."

Her head in a whirl, Alice was far too overwhelmed by the wonderful possibilities evoked by this brief phone call to even consider catching a bus to take her back to the flat. Instead, with her eyes filled with eagerness and with animation patent enough to catch the attention of passers-by, she set out briskly along Upper Street having decided to walk all the way back to the flat and to use the time this took rehearsing exactly what she was going to say to Tom if, when she got back to Aberdeen Park he hadn't, as most probably he would have, taken himself off to the pub.

She had already decided that if this Mr Solomon Kornblath was a gambler who backed plays he would certainly back Holly Wood Dresses. She had always, she told herself, known how to handle men and she must, and would, succeed with him. In any case it was not to be thought otherwise because if it wasn't so then for the rest of her life, and for the rest of Dessy and Thady's lives, nothing but disaster stretched ahead and in her state of exhilaration such an outcome was totally unacceptable.

So, setting thoughts of failure aside, she concentrated on trying to work out how best to deal with Tom, now if he was in or tomorrow morning when he'd have sobered up. She tried to remember exactly what she had said to him two hours before but only snatches came to her. That he lay in bed waited on hand and foot as if he was a member of the landed gentry. That he was getting fat and if he didn't bestir himself he would soon not even be good at games. That all he'd have in the future to buy popularity was his wretched two pounds a week pension money. That he wasn't going to stop her doing something about the mess he'd dragged them down into. That he could come home sottishly drunk and knock her about and it wouldn't make any difference – she was going to go out and make money, lots of money and if he behaved himself maybe he could come and live with her.

She paused both in thought and step. If he behaved himself! What did that mean? That providing he, to use one of his favourite expressions, toed the line, she would accept keeping him in the role of a passive layabout? Was that imaginable? She shook her head. For a short time maybe; for the long term, never! She totally lacked the patience a woman would need for that. While she was running Paquette, Sam at least had had his job and bridge and she'd been living in Belmont with all the diversions it had to offer. But in some flat – or even a house maybe when finances ran to it – living year in year out with a man still lying in bed while she set off for work, whose ambitions only stretched as far as playing games and reading books and boozing in the local? No! Unthinkable. And besides, his own pride wouldn't allow him to accept such a situation and they'd have everlasting rows and disagreements of which the children would have to bear the brunt. Anyway how could she succeed with such a millstone as he would be around her neck, everlastingly demanding his rights – not just of sex but of her time – and insisting, to use another of his damn clichés, that a man should be master in his own house. And there'd be people she'd have to meet, all sorts of people, and even when he wasn't, as he had been at first this morning, suspecting her of having an affair, he'd still be jealous of her meeting them and unable to bear the comparison of being so obviously a person of scant importance.

Could there be, she asked herself, over the years and years which stretched ahead of them, a way of successfully compromising the vastly differing interests and aspirations they would have in such a situation? She shook her head. It was all, suddenly, very clear. No, there could not be a way. It simply wouldn't work and there was no purpose in going on trying to delude herself as she had been doing through the last dreadful months. She would have quite enough to do rationing her time and energy between Holly Wood Dresses and Dessy and Thady without having to give time and energy meeting his objections, complaints and interference.

She came physically to a halt. "It's no good," she said – and she said it aloud – I have to make a decision and stick to it. I can do one of two things. Either I break away from him and set myself free to concentrate all my energies on succeeding in business and having the wherewithal to try to make up to Dessy and Thady all I've deprived them of through my two unsuccessful marriages or I risk ultimate failure through trying to carry as well the dead weight of a man who all my instincts tell me will never again hold down a job of substance. A man who, when he is faced with his own uselessness and finds it impossible to live up to the principles he sets such store by, will be impossible to live with. A man who will be consumed with jealousy whenever I lavish the love and care my children deserve from me. A man who, however much he loves me, lacks the moral strength to resist the pressures my being away all day will load on him and will inevitably turn to the bottle for solace and escape. A man who, when – to use his damn words again – the chips are down, is so incapable of self-control that he has to find relief in knocking me about or indulging in the sort of outburst I had to put up with a couple of hours ago!

And the anger which had driven her into launching into her diatribe of his faults and failings and had been quenched by elation returned, refired. Why should I have to put up with any more mornings like this morning, why should my children have to? What on earth would I lose, anyway, if I parted from him? Companionship? She shrugged companionship away. What sort of companionship was it that had to rely on guile and pretence and everlastingly turning the other cheek? Yes, I'd be lonely. There'd be empty hours – something I've never in my whole life known before. But I could use those hours – use them making up for all the hours out of which Dessy and Thady have been cheated by hotel life and boarding school.

And what would *they* lose if Tom and I part company? Absolutely nothing! Their interests are poles apart and most probably he secretly despises them because they couldn't care less about the one thing that really matters to him: games. They've nothing in common and by the time they're adults, except in the most superficial ways, he'll end up having contributed absolutely nothing to their development.

And the other side of the penny? Gain. She nodded an affirmative. Yes, there'd be gain all right. To start with they'd be spared that awful feeling of uncertainty each evening holds for them, that wondering, whether when he comes in *Pops* – and she thought the word scornfully – will be in a good humour or a ranting and raging bully, shouting and slamming doors and putting the fear of God into them! And then there's having to put up with the situation of having a man who supposed to be their father but whose name is Fenwick while theirs is Jordan. I know how embarrassing they find that, the only boys in two separate schools who so far as I know are in such a predicament. Well, I can't alter that but if they were just living with me it wouldn't be so obvious – maybe, even, I could get my name changed back to Jordan. It's what everybody knows me by in business.

She shook her head, annoyed with herself for letting these more unimportant things crowd her brain when the one real gain, a gain which surely transcended everything else, stood out a mile. That once she was parted from Tom all the love she was capable of giving could be theirs, need never again be shared with anyone else.

She was quite decided. The reasons for breaking with Tom

so far outweighed those for remaining with him as not to be argued against. All that had to be done was to choose the right moment for telling him. She had to be practical. It wasn't a simple matter of walking back into the flat and starting packing suitcases! Not with two children to be considered and these wonderful possibilities the meeting with this Kornblath man held out. She would have to be patient, endure his tantrums, soft-soap him, let him have his damn sex with her. She must do nothing, absolutely nothing, which could in the slightest way risk upsetting the Kornblath applecart.

The vital thing was to get Holly Wood Dresses launched. Once that had happened she would come to some, hopefully amicable, arrangement with him. Until then she must steel herself to patience. And when it had happened she must equally steel herself not to allow his protestations of his love for her, and the sympathy for him in his plight which she knew would threaten her resolve, to sway her from the only course which could secure Dessy and Thady's future.

5

She was not surprised to find the flat empty. The Royal Oak would be open by now and, as drink began to have its effect and before it quite befuddled his faculties, he'd be leaning against the bar spirited with righteous indignation. If he found a crony he'd be indulging in some of his everlasting clichés to do with running his own ship or being a master in his house. And at two o'clock, when the pubs had to close, he'd come back here because there was nowhere else for him to go to. He wouldn't be drunk but, as he would put it, tight, walking very carefully, persuading himself that he could carry two or three pints without it showing. And he would come down the short flight of steps and scratch around with his key before he got it fitted into the lock and then he'd come in, falsely jocund, prepared, providing he got co-operation, to let bygones be bygones but, if he didn't, ready to prove who ruled the roost in Aberdeen Park.

And to a degree she would have to go along with it. She would withdraw nothing of what she'd said, apologise for none of it but take the easy way. Offer, with bad grace, to make him lunch, an omelette perhaps. Most likely he'd turn it down but perhaps not. It depended on his mood, on who he'd been drinking with. He wouldn't ask her how she'd got on with Culverwell, not then, because to do so would be to demean himself; later, when some sort of accord had been restored between them, he would possibly raise it. It depended on how things went. Oh, what a business it was – so much sham, so much mental dishonesty, so much evasion, subterfuge, shuffling. Letters stuffed into blouses, bits of envelope poked into cisterns, Post Office books secreted at risk of being nibbled away by mice, headaches claimed which did not exist – and the everlastingly new beginnings when undying love was professed and the old promises that the weakness would be fought down made and the solemn word of honour given that she would never have to put up with it again.

It was in such a mood that Alice, going into the sitting room, spotted the envelope lying on the Jacobean table. She could have laughed aloud. I wonder, she thought, how he'll begin *this* one. Surely he won't start it like the last one, saying he wouldn't make love to me in it, that I must hate him for what he'd said, that he loathed himself for hurting me so much. Whatever it was, it would have to be in that vein. If he was still incensed with her, the last thing he would do would be to express that in a letter!

The thought brought her up short, made her wonder and even induced a shaft of guilt. She had said terrible things to him. She had been entitled to say those things and all of them were true and justified but because they were, and in his heart he knew they were, they would be doubly hurtful. He was a weak man, perhaps the weakest man she had ever known, and she had crucified him. And now she imagined him, not in a pub, not boasting to cronies, but alone, walking the streets of Islington, ashamed of what he'd done, fearful of losing her, trying to puzzle out some formula which would meet her needs and leave him with a little pride.

She reached for the envelope and with her fingernail ripped back the flap – and read.

> *My darling Micky, I have let you – and Desmond and Thady – down in word and deed but, believe me, not in thought. I wanted to give all of you the world but I have utterly failed you and in doing so failed myself. You have drawn an accurate picture of what life has in store for us if I continue to be a millstone around your neck and I cannot bear the thought of it. Nor could I accept what Sam Jordan was apparently able to accept, a way of life largely dependent on the earnings of my wife. With all my heart and soul I loved you – always remember that. I know my faults, my weaknesses – I have always known them. I had hoped with you by my side I would conquer them and lead you into the sunlit uplands of life. Instead I have dragged you down into the depths of hopelessness. Forgive me for hurting you so much but there is this devil inside me I lack the power to control. Whatever you do, do not blame yourself, nor lose too much sleep about me. Mott, who has been, if indirectly, so responsible for much of the unhappiness in your life, once accused you of being a plagiarist and you did not deny it at the time and so I am sure you will forgive me if I end, my love, by being a plagiarist myself and saying that this is a far, far better thing that I go to do, than I have*

ever done and a far, far better rest that I am going to, than I have ever known.

In some uncontrolled reaction Alice's hand, holding the letter, fell so that the knuckles actually lightly rapped the table-top and for long moments she stood motionless staring at but not seeing the bank of ivy-clad earth reaching to halfway up the window of the semi-basement flat. And then she bent her head and re-read the letter, not the whole of it, but only the last few lines, then gently folded it and placed it on the table.

Not for a moment did she fail to understand what the letter was telling her; not for a moment did she doubt that the threat implied it in would be carried out. Tom was going to kill himself – and he would do so. The principles she had mentally scoffed at on her way back along Upper Street were far too deeply ingrained in him to be set aside. She had thought of him as a coward and a coward he was, but only in certain aspects of his character. On cricket pitch and rugger field he was a lion and would have been in war. The letter was a promise; he would not renege on it. He would kill himself – perhaps had already done so.

She sat at the table, the folded letter in both hands, stunned by the shock of it yet with a hundred thoughts tumbling and jostling for precedence. And, keeping the thoughts company, so many emotions: sorrow, guilt, regret, dismay, anger, chagrin.

This didn't have to happen, she told herself, I could have stopped it happening. But for my pride I would have come back after failing to get through to Culverwell and this would not have happened.

She reflected on the thoughts which had so occupied her mind on her slow return from the the Angel and saw how precisely they fitted in with what had happened. Oh, Tom, she thought, if you had known those thoughts that I was having, how you would have smiled. If you had known those thoughts, far from being dissuaded from whatever it is that you have done or are going to do, you would have hurried to do it quicker.

She unfolded the letter and re-read it. How generous you've been, she thought. You've made all my excuses for me. And you've done something else. You've triumphed – for you have left me with a memory of you that neither time nor reflections on the bad days we've had or the bad things we've said will tarnish. Until I die you will always be a man who loved me, who would, as you have said, had it been in your power, have given me the world. You were weak and there was little in you to give but all that you had to give you've given me.

And two more things you've done: strengthened me and cleared from my path all obstacles to success. If I fail, I shall have only myself to blame, never you. And you've done something more – you've cleansed my soul of bitterness: no one, not Dessy, not Thady, not anyone, will ever hear a word from me said against you.

What do I do? she asked herself. Surely there's something I should be doing. I can't just sit here waiting, waiting for I don't know what. I must do something. Should I go round to the police station and show them your note? She shook her head. What for? There's no sense in doing that – it would be only window dressing. You've said you're going to kill yourself and kill yourself you will. I don't know how or where you're going to do it and neither will they. They wouldn't know where to start. And if, by some miracle, by telling the police I *was* able to stop you doing it, you would despise yourself for the rest of your life and be angry with me for spoiling everything just when you thought you had put it all to rights.

Unable to stay still she paced the room for a little while and then, driven to do something positive, went into the kitchen and put the kettle on only after a moment or two to wonder why she'd done so and turn the gas off again. Refusing to let her mind visualise in what way Tom might kill himself she was thinking instead only of the results of his doing so.

Someone will report finding him and will tell the police and maybe tomorrow, maybe even today, a policeman will come knocking at the door to break the news. Oh God, she prayed, when they do, please let it be at a time when Dessy and Thady are at school. She looked at the kitchen clock. They'll be home soon, she thought. Thady first and Dessy half an hour after him. Perhaps I should go to the police station after all to tell them I've two children and they're not to come here to tell me. And the thought brought to the forefront of her mind the effect Tom committing suicide might have on them. As if it hadn't been bad enough for them to have had had a father with a name different from their own, now they would have to face living with the notoriety of one who had committed suicide!

And this brought her up short, forcing her to face the only thing which in the long run really mattered: how she should handle the hours which lay immediately ahead so as to limit the scars which must inevitably be left on the minds of her two children.

How long have I got, she asked herself – and glanced at the clock again. Less than an hour. Less than an hour to decide what I'm going to tell them. They'll be wondering why Tom isn't in. They're bound to ask. How do I answer them? I can't tell them what's going to happen ahead of its happening. I'll have to think of some excuse for his not being here. And then I'll give them their tea. I know, I'll get a good fire going to welcome them and then I'll give them their tea. Thank goodness I bought those Kup Cakes yesterday. And while they're having their tea, I'll say I've got to nip out for something at the shops and I'll go to the police station at Highbury Barn and show them Tom's letter and tell them they're not to send a policeman round, that they've got to find some other way of telling me. Perhaps I should do that right away. She glanced at the clock again. No, there isn't the time; they'd be bound to keep me while they asked questions and got it all written down. No, that's what I'll do. Light a fire and give them their tea and then go and show Tom's letter to the police. That will deal with now. But what about as the hours pass and Tom still isn't home? And later? When I know it's happened? When the police have told me? She glanced at the clock for the third time. Oh, Lord, she thought – so little time to think of what to say now and how best to break it to them later. And it's so important I do it properly because if I can, then afterwards . . . Afterwards. The word steadied her as perhaps no other word could have done. Yes, there would be afterwards. That was what she must cling to through the next dreadful hours. There would be an afterwards in which for the first time in her life she would be in full control of her own destiny and in which all the love which was within her could be given entirely to Dessy and Thady. And it occurred to her that these were Tom's final gifts to her and to her children. She must not fail to use them properly. She would not fail.